DAUGHTER OF RAGE AND BEAUTY

AMY PENNZA

CHAPTER
ONE

I gazed at the forest zipping by the car window. My stomach did a lazy flip, like a slimy sea creature flopping over. Saliva pooled in my mouth. I swallowed and took shallow breaths.

It didn't help.

"Is something wrong?"

The deep, masculine voice came from the seat across from me. Its owner pegged me with a look that was somehow both bored and irritated.

I swallowed again. "Just a little car sick, my lord."

Harald Berregaard raised a white-blond eyebrow. "Car sick." His eyebrow continued to hold at a precise angle above his icy blue eyes. The pale color was striking enough on its own, but it was made even more so against the stark purity of his long, platinum hair.

He didn't like it. At least that's what the maids at Berregaard Manor whispered behind his back. "You'll never see Lord Harald with his hair unbound," they said.

They could be wrong. Servants whispered all kinds of

things. Maybe he just didn't like hair in his face. Maybe he thought the blond made him appear less warrior-like.

Or maybe he hated seeing the same coloring reflected back at him every time he looked at me.

His lips compressed in a tight line, and I realized he was waiting for me to answer.

"Yes." I cleared my throat. The car hit a bump, making my stomach slosh. "A little car sick," I finished weakly.

Disgust flickered across his features. He looked out his own window, dismissing me. "We'll be there shortly."

The creature in my stomach turned into a thousand tiny butterflies. As much as I wanted to exit the car—and his presence—the prospect of reaching our destination filled me with dread.

The car hit another bump. I gripped the seat. "Couldn't we have just opened a portal?"

This time, Harald's look was all irritation. "That you even ask such a thing is precisely why I'm sending you to Bjørneskalle, Elin."

"I didn't—"

"This penchant for cutting corners, for taking the easy way out, is most unbecoming." His voice got lower as he spoke—a sign he was truly angry. Most people yelled when they were upset. Harald Berregaard grew deadly quiet. At his most furious, he spoke in a menacing whisper. "I thought hiring an extra tutor might give you the push you needed. Clearly, I was wrong. You are determined to remain unstable, emotional, and flighty."

Like your mother. He didn't say the words, but they floated in the air nonetheless.

Anger surged in my chest—a welcome change from the nausea. "I only asked why we couldn't use a portal. I don't think that makes me flighty."

His expression didn't change. He had too much control for that. But his response was as sharp as the longsword leaning against the seat near his knee. "The Holmgang is like any other quest. When a berserker accepts a quest, he doesn't take shortcuts. This is one of the first things you should have learned."

"Then maybe you should have hired better tutors." As soon as I said it, I wanted to snatch the words back. My throat went dry, and I couldn't help glancing at his sword. A scene flickered through my mind—him pulling the blade from the scabbard and chopping my head off. Maybe he'd display it from the gates of Berregaard Manor so passersby would know not to sass the lord. Not that anyone ever did. Apparently, I was the only person stupid enough to do that.

I held my breath, waiting for him to lash out.

But he just stared, the weight of his displeasure pressing me deeper into my seat. The muscle twitching in his jaw was his only concession to rage.

Which was, of course, the reason he was revered by berserkers. Humans thought we were mystical warriors who donned animal skins and fought until we dropped. Or that we drugged ourselves into a trance-like fury so we could rage our way through battle.

Humans got it all backwards, as they did with most things involving Mythicals—the catchall name for the various races of supernaturals and immortals who made up the Myth.

Berserkers weren't human. But unlike most creatures of the Myth, we had to work for our immortality. It took a thousand kills before Odin granted us the gift of everlasting life. The kills also had to be worthy—justifiable deaths sanctioned by our leaders. We couldn't plunge mindlessly into battle and slaughter everyone in sight.

The rage part was real enough. But it was a wild magic every berserker had to learn to control. And that was where

Harald excelled above nearly every other berserker lord alive. As soon as their children were old enough to walk, berserker mothers put a sword in their hands and told them, "May you be like Lord Harald, steady and wise!"

Except my mother never told me that. She never got the chance.

The silence stretched. The fine hairs on my arms lifted as Harald continued to stare. My pulse thumped in my ears. Desperate to break the uncomfortable spell, I opened my mouth to apologize—

"My lord?" The driver's voice came from a small speaker in the panel behind my head.

Harald answered without breaking eye contact. "Yes?"

"We're approaching the gates."

"Thank you, Nils."

There was a soft click, which meant the speaker was off and Harald and I were free to resume our staring contest.

His expression shifted, the scathing disapproval replaced with something that might have been satisfaction. He settled back in his seat. "You're insolent." He gestured out the window. "Bjørneskalle will remedy that."

I followed the direction he pointed—and any reply I might have offered fled as a looming structure filled my vision.

Bjørneskalle Castle. Seat of the Rage Lords and home to the Noble Guild of Berserker Assassins. It also hosted the Holmgang—the rehabilitation program for berserkers who couldn't master their rage.

Berserkers like me.

The Holmgang was a grueling mix of training and trials. No one *wanted* to attempt it, but most were grateful for the opportunity it offered. Because there was no such thing as a "failed berserker." Those unable to control their rage were put to death. As soon as I stepped inside Bjørneskalle, I'd become a *drengr*—a participant in the program. If I failed the trials, my life was forfeit.

My heart pounded as we neared the caste. I'd seen it just once before, when I made my first offering to Odin as a child. It was just as impressive now as then. Twelve stories of weather-worn stone soared against a bright blue sky. The main keep was a rectangle with four spiraling towers at each corner. Dozens of chimneys dotted the roof, their edges adorned with grimacing gargoyles. A short distance away from the keep stood a lone, round tower. Unlike the others, this one was plain and broken, its battlements crumbling.

The Dragon Tower. Legend said it predated the keep by a thousand years. The stone was darker, the blocks rougher. Every berserker child knew the saga of the Dragon Tower. Ulfrik, the first berserker king, had built it for his dragon, Fridgeir—a fearsome beast that could fly high enough to reach Odin's hall.

Some claimed the current berserker king still rode a descendant of Fridgeir. I was more inclined to think he traveled by private jet like every other celebrity—Mythical or human. But no one had seen King Magnus in over a decade. In his absence, the Rage Lords ruled over the berserkers.

The road curved, bringing the castle wall into view. It ran the entire perimeter of the castle until it connected with the cliffs that made up Bjørneskalle Fjord. Most walls were designed to keep people out. The wall around Bjørneskalle was there to keep people in.

As the car neared the gate, a flock of birds lifted from the castle roof and wheeled into the sky. Black as night, they streaked across the blue like arrows. One broke formation, dipped to the fjord, and dragged a talon through the dark blue water, raising white spray in its wake.

"Ravens," Harald said.

When I looked at him, he was watching me, his pale eyes emotionless once more.

"They alert the Hersir when someone approaches the gate," he added, referring to the berserker who oversaw the Holmgang. "Or when a drengr dies."

I returned my gaze to the window as my stomach resumed pitching and rolling. I focused on the horizon. That was what my old nanny, Fiona, always said to do whenever I felt sick in the car. *"Just keep yer gaze on the trees, lass. Twill calm yer belly until I can get a wee biscuit in ye."*

That was her solution for everything—biscuits slathered in butter and honey. Brownies were like that—forever baking and cleaning. If I scraped my knee during sword practice, she clucked her tongue and pulled a biscuit from her apron pocket. When reciting the sagas for hours gave me headaches, she pushed a biscuit at me. The time Harald banished me from the great hall for giggling, she tapped on my door at midnight with a basket of fresh baked biscuits, cheese, and ham.

It was the only time I saw her angry. Her normally cheerful face with its upturned nose and layers of wrinkles had been scrunched into a scowl, her bright brown eyes narrowed and dull.

"What is it?" I'd said, taking the basket from her.

She'd shaken her head, her brown curls bouncing under her white cap.

I'd leaned against the jamb, my arms folded. "Fiona."

She spoke in an aggravated burst. "Punishin' a bairn for laughin'. It isnae right."

"Berserkers don't laugh."

Her anger had fled, replaced with something worn and sad. "Och. Everyone laughs, lass. Some just choose tae forget how."

The car slowed, pulling me out of my memories. We entered the gate and passed a large, green field bordered by wooden stands. In the middle of the field, several pairs of warriors sparred. Male and female, they wielded long broadswords like the one at Harald's knee. They were dressed simply in black leather pants and matching jerkins that exposed their arms.

As we passed, a young woman forced her opponent to one knee. She looked up suddenly, her gaze connecting with mine. Even with the distance between us, her amethyst eyes gleamed in her pale face. Her long, black hair was plaited around her crown before spilling down her back in a ponytail. Unlike the other fighters, her jerkin was a rich burgundy.

Her gaze narrowed. Just before the field passed out of view, she whirled, black hair swinging.

I sat back in my seat. *What was that?*

The car slowed, and I put the woman from my mind as we stopped in a stone courtyard. A second later, Nils was at my door, one fist over his chest. "Madam."

I climbed out and gave him a look. No one else at Berregaard Manor called me that. Of course, they weren't the son of a disgraced berserker who abandoned his family and ran off with a siren. Nils was desperate to rehab his family's good name, so he did whatever he could to ingratiate himself with Harald.

Sucking up to *me* wasn't the way to do it, but Nils was undeterred. I gave his shoulder a playful bump. "I thought you were coming to this place with me." Not as a drengr. Unlike me, he could control his rage. But it was customary for young berserkers to petition the Rage Lords for quests—a euphemism for "assassinations." Nils had a lot of kills to collect before he shed his mortality.

He dropped his formal expression, and the boy I remembered peeked out of his brown eyes. For a couple years, I'd thought his steady, wholesome handsomeness was what I wanted. "I wish I could, Eely," he said, using my childhood nickname. "But Lord Harald said I need permission from my dad."

"Do you know where he is?" I glanced over my shoulder. Harald stood behind the car, his black leather coat flapping around his ankles as he buckled his sword in place.

Color entered Nils' cheeks. "Somewhere in the Caribbean."

"With your stepmother?"

"With a harlot," Harald said behind me.

I turned. He watched us, his pale eyes hard. A faint breeze stirred his hair, making long white strands whip against one leather-clad elbow.

"Don't worry, son," he told Nils. "Your father isn't the first berserker to be lured by a conniving female. It's a trait common among that sex, I'm afraid."

Outrage filled me, but I bit my tongue. He wanted a reaction. I could best him simply by denying him one.

Nils averted his gaze, his dark brows pulled together.

Before Harald could say anything else, a young man strode toward us from the keep. Or at least he appeared young. With most Mythicals, it was hard to guess chronological age.

As he drew near, I decided he was probably no more than twenty. He had young eyes—and the demeanor of someone new to authority. His shoulders were just a bit too stiff, his features tinged with a hint of self-doubt—an expression I recognized from seeing it in the mirror. He was dressed like the black-haired woman, in leather pants and a burgundy jerkin.

When he reached us, he put a fist to his chest and gave a short bow. "Lord Harald, it's an honor to receive you at Bjørneskalle."

Harald returned the salute, then clapped the other man's shoulder. "It's good to be back, even if just for a short time. Are any of the other lords in residence?"

"No, my lord." The younger man hesitated. "If I'd known you wished to see them, I would have—"

"Don't mention it." Harald flicked a glance at me, and his voice tightened. "This is Elin."

The young man turned to me. "I'm Ulfar Gundersen. If you'll follow me, I'll show you to your quarters."

My heart jumped into my throat. I looked between him and Harald. "Right now?"

Ulfar spoke as if he hadn't heard the panic in my voice. "You're permitted one bag." He glanced at Nils. "Your man here can leave it in the courtyard. Someone will fetch it after it's been inspected."

They were going to search my stuff? Things were moving too fast. I hadn't expected to start the Holmgang right away.

Nils fetched my duffel from the trunk and set it on the ground.

"This way," Ulfar said. He turned on his heel and started toward the castle.

"Wait!" The plea burst from me before I could stop it.

He stopped and gave me a perplexed look over his shoulder.

I looked at Harald, all my anger and resentment draining away at the prospect of walking into Bjørneskalle alone. "What about the oath-taking?"

"What about it?"

"Aren't you staying for it?"

"I've matters to attend to at the manor. Petitions and such."

That was more important than watching me take a blood oath? Out of the corner of my eye, I saw Nils lower his head.

A little voice urged me to shut up and follow Ulfar. But I couldn't. I stepped closer to Harald. "It's my first oath. I'm taking a vow to die if I fail the Holmgang."

He put a hand on his sword hilt. The silence stretched. When he spoke at last, his voice was hard. "Then I suggest you don't fail."

I sucked in a breath. For a second, my throat burned.

Then the burning...shifted.

All at once, there was a ball of energy in my chest—a small, seething sun that destroyed itself and then formed anew. Each time, it swelled larger. Grew more unstable. I gritted my teeth. My skin ached.

Somewhere in the distance, lightning struck. The sky behind the castle flared white, the clouds forked with electricity.

My hair lifted away from my head, the platinum waves floating as if suspended underwater. My body was frozen. Thunder boomed.

"*Elin.*" The voice came from far away. As if it, too, was underwater. But it was a kind voice. In some dim, foggy corner of my brain, I recognized it.

The ball contracted, becoming smaller and more concentrated. More dangerous.

I clenched my fists. Energy sizzled along my veins. I stared at Harald. I couldn't have looked away if I tried.

He regarded me with his usual detachment, his gaze disinterested.

More lightning flashed. A second later, thunder shook the ground. The power was too much for me to hold. Like a snake flicking its tongue, it tested the air, seeking release.

"Elin!" The voice again. Louder this time.

I tried to turn my head, but the power held me immobile. My skin burned. My eyes bulged in their sockets.

"ELIN!"

Something struck my shoulder. I stumbled sideways. The

spell broke, and the ball imploded. Energy unraveled, dissipating into the air.

I staggered, and my hip bumped the car. I leaned against the warm metal as my heart galloped in my chest.

Nils' worried face filled my vision. "Are you okay?"

For a second, I wanted nothing more than to throw myself at him. To feel the familiar comfort of strong arms and a broad chest. But we weren't in the barn at Berregaard Manor. It wasn't a lazy summer day, and we weren't sixteen anymore.

"Yes." My voice emerged as a rasp, so I cleared my throat and tried again. "Yes. Thank you, Nils."

His big hands twitched like he might reach for me. But then he seemed to catch himself, and he eased back and nodded.

I straightened. Harald and Ulfar watched me, twin looks of disapproval on their faces. I hadn't even started the Holmgang and I was already failing.

Harald looked at Ulfar. "I leave her in your hands. As you can see, she has few redeeming qualities."

Ulfar inclined his head.

"Give your father my regards." Harald swept his coat around his body and turned toward the car. Nils sprang into action and opened the door.

At the mention of his father, Ulfar's expression brightened. "I will, my lord. He just celebrated his thousandth kill."

Harald froze, his shoulders taut. Slowly, he faced Ulfar "Is that so?"

"Yes, sir. Just last month."

"Well." Harald's smile didn't reach his eyes. "A long life to him, then."

"Yes, my lord. Thank you."

Harald tucked his sword against his leg and climbed into the car. Nils shut the door behind him and turned to me, his eyes anxious. "You sure you're okay?"

The car window lowered halfway. "Nils." Harald's voice was sharp. "I don't want to delay."

"I'm fine," I told Nils.

His expression said he didn't believe me, but he put his fist over his heart and offered me a bow. "Farewell, Elin."

I repeated the gesture. "Farewell, Nils."

He spoke under his breath. "Give 'em hell, Eely." He spun and hurried around the front of the car.

I was still smiling when the feeling of being watched made my skin prickle. I turned my head.

Harald regarded me, his eyes cold. Being seated meant he was forced to look up to meet my gaze.

Nils started the car.

Few redeeming qualities.

The lower half of the window reflected my face, showing my platinum hair and ice blue eyes.

Harald faced forward, dismissing me.

As the car pulled away, I put my fist over my heart and made a mocking bow.

"Farewell, Father."

CHAPTER

TWO

The inside of the castle was just as impressive as the outside—and as big as I remembered. The ceilings soared overhead, and the walls were decorated with statues and gilt framed paintings. I could have spent hours looking at them.

But Ulfar wasn't interested in being a tour guide.

I lengthened my stride to keep up with him as he ascended the steps leading to a set of massive wooden doors. The site of them jogged my memory.

The Great Hall. Legend said it was the largest in Europe, its iron chandeliers lit with everlasting flames blown to life by ifrits. When I'd made my offering to Odin, I'd spent most of the time staring at the strange, mesmerizing light. My childhood visit to Bjørneskalle was largely a blur, but the Great Hall stuck in my mind like someone had placed a photograph there.

Ulfar reached the top of the stairs and made a sharp left, bypassing the doors.

"Hey!" I panted as I gained the top two steps.

He stopped and turned. "What is it?"

I gestured to the Hall. "Aren't we going inside?"

He glanced at the doors, which were decorated with carved runes and rows of iron studs. "No."

"But the oath-taking." Surely something as important as a blood oath had to take place in the Great Hall?

"It'll have to wait. The Hersir presides over all oaths, and he's away right now."

At the mention of the Hersir, an image of an old, bearded man popped into my head. Which was most likely inaccurate. Berserkers aged slowly—and not at all once we achieved immortality.

And the Hersir *had* to be immortal. The Rage Lords wouldn't put a mortal in charge of the Holmgang. The program was too important. Berserkers weren't exactly a prolific species to begin with, but we were also incredibly important to the Mythical world. Because our kills had to be worthy, we took on the challenge of eliminating immortals who went mad or threatened to expose our existence to humans. By the time a creature of the Myth reached that point, they had amassed almost god-like power. Some had even been worshipped as gods by humans in the past. That made them extremely hard to kill.

The Rage Lords made a lot of money sending their berserkers to do the job, and they had a vested interest in keeping their warriors alive.

Which was why they'd given me a second chance.

Holmgang meant "duel" but the rehabilitation program didn't pit failed berserkers against each other. I wouldn't be fighting an opponent. As I had in the courtyard, I'd be wrestling with my own magic.

And the Hersir was the only person with the authority to say whether I succeeded.

"When will he be back?" I asked Ulfar. "Is he on vacation or something?"

He looked at me like I'd grown an extra head. "You talk like a human."

I shrugged. It was either that or tell him he walked like he had a stick up his ass.

Our exchange must have loosened him up, though, because he cleared his throat. "Back at the car... Lord Harald seemed angry with me just before he left."

Ah. So Ulfar was more perceptive than he looked. "Probably because you mentioned your father getting a thousand kills. Harald's sensitive about his mortality." Which was putting it mildly. "Obsessed" might be a better way to describe it. Or maybe "maniacal."

Ulfar frowned. "Why doesn't he just accept more quests?"

I had no idea. Harald and I weren't exactly confidants. "He's busy, I guess. I think he's somewhere in the eight hundreds now. We used to have a big celebration after each one, but that stopped when—" I snapped my mouth shut.

"When what?"

I shook my head. They'd stopped when Fiona died. "We just don't have them anymore."

His expression lost some of its sternness. And when he resumed leading me through the castle, he slowed his pace.

The corridor leading away from the Great Hall was broad, its walls dotted with artwork and the occasional door. Every dozen steps or so, it branched off into another passageway. Most were simple arches, but some were flanked by columns or even statues.

We'd walked for about five minutes when we came upon the fanciest one yet. An ornate archway was supported by two stone figures—tall, dour-looking men with long beards, each one clutching the hilt of a broadsword in front of his chest. The arch they guarded led to a set of steps.

As we passed, the little hairs on my nape lifted. I looked up.

The statue on the right had turned its head toward me, and its carved eye sockets now glowed a dull blue.

I stumbled to a halt. "Ulfar."

He stopped, then followed my gaze. "Those are the Norsemen."

I swallowed. "That one is staring at me."

"It's just doing its job."

"The statues here have jobs?"

"Not all of them." He gestured toward the steps beyond the arch. "These guard the entrance to the Hersir's Tower. They only allow those with permission to enter."

"What happens if you try to go in without permission?"

He frowned. "I wouldn't do that."

The statue seemed to decide I wasn't about to try it, because it turned its head back to its original position. The blue glow dimmed, then died entirely.

"Come on," Ulfar said.

I followed quickly, and I didn't breathe easy until we'd rounded the corner.

It wasn't long before I wondered if the Holmgang had already started and Ulfar was trying to test my endurance. As we climbed staircase after staircase, the muscles in my legs burned like fire.

"How much farther?" I asked on what had to be the hundredth set of stairs.

"Just up here," he said over his shoulder. Of course, *he* sounded fine. He even bounded up the last step and waited for me on a landing lit by a large mullioned window, its panes wavy with age.

When I hauled myself over the threshold, he pointed down a short hallway lined with doors. "Maya thought you'd be happier away from the others."

Away? As in isolated? Dozens of questions buzzed through my head. I settled on the one that seemed most important. "Who's Maya?"

"A Proven, as I am."

So that was why he was in charge of showing me around. He was nearly finished with the Holmgang. Now it was just a short jump—and a worthy kill—to being a full-fledged berserker.

And he got to live.

Apparently, being a Proven also meant you could discriminate against half-breeds. "Is Maya the woman with the long black ponytail?"

"You've met her?"

"Sort of. She thought I'd be happier by myself?"

Two faint spots of color appeared high on his cheekbones. But he held my gaze. "Because you're a nymph."

Ice slid down my spine. "I'm half Fae. I didn't think that was a disqualification for attempting the Holmgang."

"It's not." For a moment, it seemed like he might say more, but then he tugged his jerkin down in a crisp motion. "Your room is the second on the left." Before I could react, he saluted and headed down the stairs.

"Wait!" I called after him. "When do I start my trials? Is there a schedule?" My questions bounced off the walls.

He stopped. Barely turning his head, he muttered, "Someone will wake you in the morning." He straightened and started down the hall, his boots ringing sharply against the stone.

I slumped against the wall, my gaze on the flagstones. *"Because you're a nymph,"* he'd said, the last uttered in the tone people used when discovering dog shit on the bottom of their shoe. I should have expected it, but somehow I hadn't. Maybe living at Berregaard Manor had made me soft. There, no one cared where my mother came from. Hell, most of the staff were Mythicals with sketchy family trees—

I lifted my head.

That was it. I'd spent my childhood surrounded by servants. Aside from the string of berserker tutors Harald had hired over the years, every other being on the estate had been part of the household staff. Humans thought their societies were divisive and stratified, but they had nothing on the creatures that made up the Myth. Half-breeds were common among the servant class, which wasn't as obsessed with bloodlines as the more "noble" races.

I'd been sheltered at the manor. Now the real world was slapping me in the face.

Damp from the stone seeped through my sweater and reached my skin. I pushed off the wall, then climbed the steps back to the landing. Sunlight poured through the window, making bright shapes on the stone floor. I did a slow turn in the hallway, my gaze wandering. For an attic, it wasn't so bad. The ceilings were arched like those in a cathedral, and fluted columns were built into the walls around the doors. Lanterns were spaced evenly along the ceiling. I craned my head back and squinted. Were they lit by ifrit fire, too?

Nope. Just regular light bulbs. Apparently, not even the Rage Lords were wealthy enough to power their whole castle with neverending flame.

I went to the second door on the left and stopped. The wood was stained dark, but the spruce underneath was unmistakable. I put my palm flat on the surface and closed my eyes. Immediately, images flashed through my head.

Men in bowl-shaped helmets and short red tunics. Running. Screaming. Rectangular shields discarded in the mud. Yelling. Snow swirling. Through the white haze, a golden eagle hoisted on a pole.

I opened my eyes. The wood warmed under my hand. "The Roman Republic, huh?" I patted it. "You've seen a lot, old friend."

Friend. A smile tugged at my lips. Maybe I had allies in the castle, after all.

I gave the door another gentle pat, then lifted the latch and walked inside.

"Spartan" was an understatement. Aside from a beautiful window that filled the space with light, the rest of the room was as stark as a prison cell. There was a large fireplace— nearly big enough to stand in—but the grate was dark and cold. One wall held a chair and desk, another a narrow twin bed covered by a gray blanket. I walked to it and ran my fingertips over the material.

Wool. Fabulous.

The opposite wall was dominated by an arched nook covered with a curtain that was half pulled aside. I walked to it and peeked in. Leather pants and jerkins hung in a row, each set black as night.

At least they weren't orange jumpsuits.

On the floor were two pairs of military boots. I suppressed a groan.

My ankles were going to *hate* Bjørneskalle.

There was no bathroom. That was probably down the hall somewhere. At least my tainted nymph blood meant I probably wouldn't have to share it.

My stomach growled. I'd skipped breakfast, and my queasiness on the trip had prevented me from asking Harald to stop for lunch. Not that he would have. He despised mingling with humans.

Almost as much as he despised his half-breed daughter.

A knock on the door shot through the room like a cannon blast.

I spun so quickly my head swam. Ulfar again? Or maybe Maya come to tell me I was unwelcome in Bjørneskalle.

The knock rang out again—a sharp rapping that seemed to vibrate my bones.

"I'm coming!" I hurried to the door, irritation buzzing through me. The knocking grew louder and more rapid.

I yanked the door open. "What is—" My anger melted like ice in the sun.

A satyr stood in the doorway.

And he held a basket of dinner rolls.

THREE

"Uncle Ash?"

My sole relative on my mother's side grinned and tugged at one of the brown curls spilling over his forehead. "At your service, fair Elin."

Happiness was like a firework shooting off in my chest. I laughed and jumped into his arms.

He caught me, then staggered back and let out a grunt. "Oof, you've put on weight."

I balled my fist and punched him in the ribs.

He chuckled. "Pax, shieldmaiden. Let an old jester have his fun."

"You brought food!" My stomach rumbled again.

"Of course I brought food. Eating is one of life's greatest pleasures." He hefted me higher in his arms, walked us into the room, and lowered me to the ground. Mouth next to my ear, he murmured something in a low, lilting tongue. For the briefest second, I thought I heard bells tinkling. He held me away from him and let his leaf-green gaze roam over my face.

"Ah, Elin, you wear beauty like a crown."

Spoken like a true satyr. "You have pine sap in your hair."
That wasn't unusual. But he also smelled like... I wrinkled my
nose. "Is that diesel exhaust?"

He closed the door, then went to the desk and set his
basket down. "Yeah, sorry. A bunch of Berkeley students were
protesting a logging operation so I joined in. We chained
ourselves to the Redwoods." He shrugged. "You can never have
enough tree humpers."

"It's tree *huggers*."

He grinned. "Oh, trust me we did both."

I shook my head. "Why didn't you tell me you were in
Berkeley? I tried calling you like a hundred times! That woman
you were living with in Los Angeles said she didn't know
where you were."

This time, his smile was self-deprecating. He stuffed his
hands in his jeans pockets. The cuffs of his button down shirt
were rolled up, revealing the swirl of blue pagan tattoos on his
forearms. "She kicked me out. For no reason, I might add. She
should have thanked me, considering I gave her the best sex of
her—"

"Asher." I held up a hand.

"Ah, right." He made a zipping motion across his mouth.
An assortment of necklaces adorned his neck—metal and
leather chains of various lengths. Underneath, more dark blue
tattoos decorated his chest and collarbones. With his artfully
ripped jeans, tousled hair, and head-turning good looks, he
could have come straight from a runway in Milan.

He was also barefoot.

"How did you get past the gate? These people have
swords."

His form rippled. In a blink, the handsome man was gone.
In his place stood a short, plump female with skin the color of
teak.

A lump formed in my throat. I faced away, and I had to swallow a couple times before I could speak. "Please change back."

Warm hands covered my shoulders and pulled me around. Asher tugged me against his chest. "Elin." His voice was soft and filled with regret. The scent of pine and fresh rain teased my nose. "Forgive me. I didn't realize how much you still miss her."

Stupid tears burned my eyes. "It didn't occur to me that she might die."

His chest lifted in a sigh. "Brownies aren't like us, love." He stroked my hair. "Their time on this plane is short, even if we wish it were otherwise."

I do wish it. But it did no good to rail against something I couldn't change. That was what he'd told me the night Fiona died. He'd walked into my bedroom without warning, dew threaded through his curls, and shooed the maids from the room. Then he'd climbed onto my bed and enfolded me in a hug that smelled of sun and forest.

When I'd finally stopped crying around dawn, he smoothed his fingertips over my lids, taking away the puffiness.

"Why?" My voice had come out as a croak. "Why would she leave me?"

His eyes, usually dancing with merriment, had grown distant. A long silence had stretched, and for a moment I thought he wouldn't answer. But then he'd spoken in a sad, quiet voice. "I wish I knew, child. I wish I could tell you why lovely things die...or choose to leave us."

And I'd known he was no longer talking about Fiona.

Now, I stepped out of his arms and wiped at my eyes. "I'm sorry. Some berserker I am, crying on my first day at Bjør-neskalle."

He went to my bed and sat. "You'll do fine." He jerked a thumb over his shoulder. "The door likes you."

"No one else does. They assigned me this room because I'm part nymph."

His gaze darkened. "You don't have to stay here. You could always come live with me."

I managed not to snort. "You spent six months living in a sandcastle in Greece."

"*Near* a sandcastle. And I only did it because that mermaid needed help getting rid of her ex-boyfriend." He let his eyes drift shut, like he was savoring a memory. "Mmm, she was something. Almost worth putting up with that fish tail."

I cleared my throat.

He opened his eyes, and he had the good grace to look sheepish. "Sorry. I'm just saying, why put yourself through this? Why not tap into your Fae side?"

"I'd be a horrible nymph." Not to mention I had no desire to flirt with every being I saw. There was a reason my mother's people were called the "hookers of the Fae." I couldn't say that to Asher, though.

But he must have discerned my thoughts, because he gave me a shrewd look. "There's more to being a nymph or satyr than sex, you know. Although, the sex is a pretty good perk."

I put my hands over my ears. "What was that? I can't hear you."

"Elin." He stood, his face abruptly serious.

Oh no. He was using his official uncle voice. I lowered my hands. "Is this the part where you lecture me about being judgmental?"

He folded his arms, exposing more of his tattoos. He also wore half a dozen beaded bracelets, but they weren't a fashion statement. Like most Fae, he derived energy from trees and other living things. I'd seen him weep when the news aired a story about rainforests being burned to make way for farmland. Like the door, wooden jewelry still contained a spark of life. He could probably go without some type of plant or wood touching his skin, but it would be difficult for him to do so—sort of like a human walking through waist-high water. It could be done, but it was far easier to use a bridge.

Now, he shook his head. "Just reminding you that being Fae is nothing to be ashamed of."

I opened my mouth, then shut it.

"What?"

"Nothing."

He sighed. "You know I'll pester you until you tell me."

"It's just that you and my mother..."

His eyes softened. "Yes?"

"You're lesser Fae. I mean, I don't think of you that way, but there's no denying the rest of the Myth does. It's not fair, and it's definitely not right. You're just as important as any major Fae. And who decided who's a major or lesser Fae, anyway? It's like human royalty. The whole system is just made up nonsense so some people can feel more important than others. It's ridiculous to even—"

"Elin." He held up his hands, mirth dancing in his eyes. "Take a breath before you pass out."

"You're not offended?"

"Not in the least. You think I haven't heard all this before? I'm old, sweetheart. One of the privileges of age is not caring what other people think."

Relief washed over me. I leaned against the desk. "I know. It's just that I never really thought about it before. And then today..."

"You felt that discrimination directed at you," he said.

"Yes." A bubble of humorless laughter rose in my chest.

"What's stupid is I suck at being Fae almost as much as I suck at being a berserker."

He tsked. "Now, I know that's not true." He ran a light gaze over me. "How's your glamour?"

Of course he had to ask that. Only the Fae could change their appearance at will. It was what allowed him to mimic Fiona. Even humans knew of the Fae ability to shapeshift. Children's stories were filled with tales of changelings—Fae offspring swapped for human infants. Fiona always pinned such tricks on the major Fae, who reproduced sparingly and itched to increase their numbers with more fertile humans. They couldn't really steal children anymore, though. Not with social media. All it took was one seemingly human child manifesting strange powers or sprouting pointed ears, and all of the Myth would be exposed.

As far as I knew, no Fae had pulled a changeling stunt in over a century. Although, there were a couple of ageless celebrities that made me wonder...

Asher gave me an expectant look. "Well?"

I heaved a sigh. "My glamour is non-existent."

"That's not possible. Caitríona's glamour was her strongest magic." He pronounced my mother's name the Gaelic way, with a rolled R that conjured images of bonfires and the wild hunt.

That was another thing humans got wrong. Satyrs and nymphs were associated with Greek mythology, but the Fae didn't dwell on the same plane as human beings. They certainly didn't limit themselves to geographical boundaries. Asher and my mother went by different names in different cultures. Like most Fae, Asher was tight-lipped about his age and real name. But he spoke fondly of the British Isles ("the trees there just *get* me") and he often stayed in Dublin when he chose to live among humans.

My mother had been the same, slipping in and out of the human world when it suited her. For a time, she'd even worked as a model, using glamour to achieve a perfect appearance long before Photoshop.

Asher didn't have to tell me about her skill. I'd seen how she mesmerized audiences on the catwalk. Videos of her modeling were hard to come by, since Harald had pressured her to stop working after they married.

I looked at Asher now, anger at Harald's high-handedness rising in my gut. "She could have had a brilliant career."

"Maybe." His smile held an edge of sadness that squeezed my heart. "But she couldn't have done it forever. Eventually, people would have noticed she wasn't aging."

"But she could have made herself appear older. You've done that before."

"Sure. It takes effort, though. Holding a form for a long period of time is exhausting. Most Fae just disappear for a few decades until a new crop of humans are born." He made a face. "It's harder to do these days with cameras and the internet."

I thought that over. "Maybe that explains why Odin has stayed out of sight all this time." As one of the High Fae, he held mythical status even among Mythicals. No one really knew the extent of his powers. But he hadn't been seen in twenty years. Some claimed it was because the High Fae hated technology, which interfered with magic.

"Could be," Asher said. "Maybe your King Magnus is with him. Come to think of it, you berserkers are a little light in the leadership department these days."

"The Hersir isn't here, either."

He raised an eyebrow. "Then who's going to administer your oath?"

"I don't know. They didn't exactly give me a welcome packet when I arrived." Out of nowhere, the gravity of my predicament rushed over me. Bjørneskalle wasn't a quaint castle, and the Holmgang wasn't a game. My life was on the line.

He came to me and tipped my chin up. "Hey. Everything is going to be just fine, okay?"

I smiled—or at least attempted to. Judging from the worried look on his face, it wasn't very convincing. I forced levity into my voice. "It's not a big deal. I'm not in any rush to take a blood oath anyway."

The worried look on his face deepened. "Are you sure this is necessary? You're a half-breed. We can't be certain your immortality is linked to your berserker half."

"It is. I'm aging." If I'd been a pureblooded Fae like him, I could have skipped out of Bjørneskalle and lived happily ever after—forever. But I was Harald's daughter, too, and there was enough of his blood running through my veins to put a condition on my immortality. Until I got a thousand kills, I was mortal. Vulnerable. So I had no choice about the Holmgang. Without it, I'd die anyway.

"You're twenty-one years old," Asher said. He turned my face to the side like he was looking for wrinkles. "How can you tell you're aging?"

Good question. How did I know I was like Harald instead of my mother? I shook my head. "It's just a feeling. I don't know how to describe it. But I'm sure I'm right. Assuming I can get through the Holmgang, I'm doomed to spend the next few decades working as a contract killer."

"Not a killer, Elin. More like a magical detective."

"Berserkers don't solve crimes. We flat out murder people."

"Only when they need murdering."

I started to protest, but he put a gentle finger over my lips. "No, hear me out. Mythicals live a long time, and not all of us are good. Worse, immortality can lead to boredom. When a

Mythical is inclined toward evil, boredom and a long lifespan make dangerous bedfellows." He stepped back. "The world is already a chaotic place. Imagine what it would be like without the Noble Guild of Berserker Assassins."

He spun in a tight circle. When he faced me again, it wasn't as Asher Greenleaf. Now, a taller, more muscular man stood in his place, his dark brown hair shaved on the sides and long on the top. His full beard was several shades darker than his hair, and his blue eyes had a dreamy quality to them—as if he spent a lot of time staring at a distant horizon. But it was the sword hilt peeking over his shoulder that made me recognize him.

King Magnus. I'd never seen him in person, but I didn't need to. His sword, Eldurvæng, was as recognizable as the Dragon Tower. Berserker children played with replicas of it. Harald kept a painting of it in his study.

The hilt was studded with a huge ruby, its center a swirling mix of blood red and gold rumored to have been set by Odin himself.

Magnus spoke in a deep rumble. "Being a berserker doesn't make you a killer, Elin. We are the ones who swing the sword of justice. The Myth depends on our Guild to rid the immortal races of those who would expose our secrets and sully our good names."

He made assassination-for-hire sound appealing. It didn't hurt that he was a hottie. A little solemn for my taste, but there was no denying his sex appeal.

Except wait. This wasn't King Magnus. It was my lothario uncle who'd once seduced an entire family of banshees—daughter, mother, and grandmother—all in the same week. "Thanks for the inspirational speech." I made a little spinning motion with my finger. "Now change back."

King Magnus gave me a cheeky grin, which was *weird.* Then he made a deep bow. When he straightened, he was

Asher again. He shook himself like a dog after a bath. "Eesh, he's a tough one. Lots of, um, bulk. I might have to use him the next time I'm in the States for spring break."

I bit the inside of my cheek so I didn't tell him how inappropriate it was for a centuries-old Fae to fraternize with human college students. Mythicals didn't play by the normal rules. In his case, there weren't really *any* rules.

And that was why I could never embrace my nymph side. Not only did I lack glamour and the handful of other lesser Fae abilities, I could never devote myself to an endless pursuit of pleasures of the flesh. While I didn't consider myself a prude, I just couldn't be okay with using my face and body to seduce anyone who crossed my path.

So that left me learning how to "swing the sword of justice" whenever a Mythical needed killing. My tutors claimed I had a great deal of raw power...but it was useless if I couldn't channel it. Like a sports car with no driver, I would eventually crash—but not before I caused a lot of destruction.

The Rage Lords would stop me before I got to that point. And "stop" was just a euphemism for death.

"I don't like that look," Asher said, moving closer.

"What look?"

"Defeat." He tugged on a lock of hair that had fallen over my shoulder. "It's not like you to give up so easily."

"I'm not giving up. But this is my last chance to prove myself."

He smiled. "No pressure, right?"

He expected me to laugh, so I did. Except it emerged as a sob.

Before the sound fully left my lips, he'd wrapped his arms around me. "You're tougher than you know, and there are many types of strength. I know I'm just a randy old satyr, but I'm really good at pretending to be wise."

My laugh was muffled against his shirt. Although I couldn't see his smile, I heard it in his voice.

"Years ago, when humans still carried swords, men would give everything they possessed to own a Damascus blade. They were strong enough to cleave a lesser sword in half. Clearly, a superior weapon in every way, wouldn't you say?"

I nodded.

"Ah, but here's the thing. Damascus steel could also bend. Other blades were rigid. Uncompromising. The deadliest swords in the world were also the only ones that bent without breaking. They were delicate looking things—until you had the misfortune of being on the pointed end of one."

I lifted my head from his chest.

He cupped his hands around my face, his green eyes full of fondness. "The strongest weapons bend without breaking, Elin. It doesn't make them weak."

I put my hands over his. "Thank you."

He dropped a kiss on my forehead, and the scent of honeysuckle teased my nose. As he pulled away, he murmured something under his breath in the same musical language he'd used before. As he spoke, electricity danced over my skin like champagne running through my veins. It warmed me from the inside out, tickling my face and making me laugh.

"What was that?" I asked, rubbing my nose.

But he just winked and walked backwards to the door, somehow sensing when to skirt the bed. "Call whenever you need me."

I braced my hands on my hips. "You promise you'll answer your phone this time?"

"Promise." He reached the door and opened it, then brushed a loving hand over the wood. "You can ask Old Man Spruce here, too. He knows how to reach me."

"Good to know, but I'll probably just text your cell."

"Fair enough, niece of mine." He gave me another wink, then slipped out the door.

~

FOR A WHILE, I LEANED AGAINST THE DESK, MY GAZE ON THE DOOR. If Maya wanted me isolated, she'd done a good job. I was most definitely alone.

With a sigh, I faced the desk. The food basket waited, the aromas still wafting from the white napkin folded over the top. But my appetite was gone.

Asher had brought sunshine and spring with him. I missed it already.

As if on autopilot, my hand went to my back pocket. I pulled out the desk chair as I withdrew a small, round pocket mirror. The case was silver, its surface engraved with roses and curving vines.

I sat with the mirror cupped in my palm, my thumb tracing a tiny thorn.

It was the only gift Harald had ever given me.

The metal warmed in my hand. At the same time, a soft noise filled the room—the rustle of trees tossed by the wind.

I flicked the mirror open. For a moment, my reflection stared back at me. Then my face blurred. Slowly, another took its place. The rustling grew louder.

Where my face had been, a woman came into focus.

She's in the forest.

She wasn't always. Sometimes, she stood in a vineyard. Other times, she sat on a barstool in a modern-looking kitchen.

I liked that one the best. It felt more real somehow.

But I didn't get to pick the scenery.

The image grew clearer. She sat on a tree stump, one palm braced on the wood while she gazed at something on the ground. Her long brown hair spilled down her back in a riot of soft curls. The white flower tucked behind her ear matched her simple dress, which draped over the side of the stump and trailed on the leaf-strewn forest floor.

The wind picked up, tugging at the material. She turned and looked over her shoulder.

Straight at me.

Her green eyes widened. Then her full, pink lips curved in a delighted smile. A becoming blush entered her cheeks. "Elin!" She stood and brushed leaves off her lap, laughing. "Look at me, such a mess." She lifted her gaze. "How are you?"

"I'm—" My voice was hoarse. I cleared my throat and tried again. "I'm good."

Her smile was like the sun appearing from behind a cloud. "I'm so happy to hear it." She gazed at me, love in her eyes. "Oh, I've missed you, sweetheart."

My throat ached. "I missed you too, Mom."

She gathered up her skirt and sat on the stump. "You must tell me what you've been up to. I want to hear everything." She tilted her head, her expression open and patient. Sunlight played over her face, making her skin glow.

"I'm at Bjørneskalle. I'm doing the Holmgang."

"That's wonderful! Tell me more."

Words gathered in my mind, but I held them back, my lips pressed together. In the forest, the leaves stilled as the wind died down. On my side of the mirror, silence gathered in the room, its presence almost like a distant buzz in my ears.

My mother waited, her patient expression unchanged. She was movie star stunning, with high cheekbones and a delicate jaw and nose. Her rich, dark hair was threaded with reddish highlights that caught the sun, and her skin was that rare kind of pale that looked radiant instead of sickly. Tall and curvy, her figure would have turned heads in any era.

And, of course, it had. It had turned Harald's, and he'd never forgiven her for it.

"I don't like it here," I blurted. "I'm worried I'm going to fail." I gripped the mirror and lowered my voice. "I'm bad at everything. I can't even open a portal."

My mother nodded. "I'm glad you told me." Her face brightened, as if she'd just had an idea. "I want to share something with you. May I?"

Disappointment washed over me—but only for a second. Because I knew this conversation. We'd had it hundreds of times.

She was going to sing the song.

"I'm going to sing you a song," she said, her eyes dancing.

I plastered a smile on my face, even though it didn't matter. And I said "I'd love to hear it" even though that didn't matter, either.

She sat up straighter. After a nervous laugh, she began to sing, her soprano pure and clear.

Ash and oak and willow, three
Which one shall my dearest be?
Oh, ash with leaves the first to fall
And ancient oak, its branches tall
Still willow weeps for Babylon
And forgotten times once here, now gone
Each one so very dear to me
Yet ash with fruit that holds the key

As the last few notes died in the air, she gave me a shy smile. "Well? Did you like it?"

I cupped the mirror in both hands, my heart heavy. "I loved it."

The flush in her cheeks deepened. "It sounds better in Gaelic."

"Yes. I remember."

She stood, then looked down at her dress and let out a self-conscious laugh. "Look at me!" She brushed leaves off her lap. "Such a mess."

The weight on my heart tugged harder. "I should probably go."

"Oh!" She brought her head up. "But you must tell me what you've been up to! I want to hear everything."

I smiled as my throat grew thick. "Next time."

"Of course." She lifted her arms away from her sides and tilted her head back, letting the sun shine directly on her face. In her white gown, surrounded by tall, ancient-looking trees, she resembled a pagan goddess.

Which, on some level, was exactly what she was.

"Bye, Mom."

She lowered her head. "Goodbye, Elin. Make sure you spend some time outdoors. It's so beautiful."

"I will."

"Good." She beamed at me for a second, then blew me a kiss.

My reflexes kicked in, and I pretended to catch it.

She didn't react. She just continued gazing forward, a soft smile on her lips.

I put my fingers on the back of the mirror, hesitated, and then closed it. The metal cooled against my skin. For a brief moment, I had an urge to open it again—to see if she was still standing near the stump.

But she wouldn't be. The spell didn't work that way. The mirror just reset itself, running the script from the beginning.

It was a top level enchantment. Few witches could make something so intricate. But like all magic, it had its limits. As the witch who'd taught me defensive maneuvers had been fond of saying, magic could kill in a thousand ways, but there was no enchantment strong enough to erase death.

I stood and stuffed the mirror back in my pocket. At least I hadn't put it in my duffel. Something told me Ulfar would have confiscated it.

Exhaustion swept me. I trudged to the bed and lay on my back. Using the mirror had been a mistake. I should have known it wouldn't make me feel better.

Wood creaked, and I turned my head toward the door. The faint sound of tinkling bells—so soft I had to strain to hear it—jingled in the room. Asher's voice whispered on the air. *"Bend without breaking."*

Some of the warmth I'd felt in his presence swirled around me, banishing the castle's chill.

The bells tinkled again—quieter this time—and his voice seemed to come from farther away. *"Also, I forgot to pay my phone bill, so just use the door for now."*

I snorted softly.

Not a very berserker sound. But as Asher said, I had no reason to be ashamed of my mixed heritage. There were worse things than being a nymph.

Now I just had to prove I was worthy of being a berserker.

I didn't have a choice.

As dread threatened to creep back in, I pushed it away. Tomorrow would be better.

It had to be.

It wasn't like things could get any worse.

CHAPTER

FOUR

T he next day, things got worse.

Wind gusted across the practice field, raising goosebumps on my arms and tugging at my ponytail. I folded my arms over my jerkin.

The stiff material rode up my torso, exposing my midsection.

I hunched my shoulders. Except now I could see straight down my chest, my bra more gray than white in the dreary predawn light. In this remote part of Norway, it wasn't unusual to see blizzards in November.

"Is something wrong?"

Ulfar's voice brought my head up. He stood a few paces away, a frown on his face and a broadsword in his hand.

I squared my shoulders. "No."

"You look cold."

"Because it's cold."

He slashed his sword through the air a couple times, warming up his wrists. "You think berserkers only accept quests in the summer?"

I clenched my jaw. "Do you know what my schedule is today?" Or *any* day. He'd pounded on my door an hour ago, ordered me to report to the practice field, and then promptly left. Cursing and shivering, I'd stumbled out of my room—and over my duffel, which he'd left directly in front of the door. Heaping fresh curses on him, I'd limped down the hall and found a (mercifully modern) bathroom, where I'd showered in record time and shoved my damp hair into a ponytail.

The wind gusted harder, trailing icy fingers across my skin.

Ulfar whipped the sword in an infinity pattern around his body, his biceps taut from the effort.

I tilted my head. Apparently, the modicum of goodwill I'd established with him yesterday had been imaginary, and he was back to being a total asshole instead of *mostly* an asshole. Just when I thought he was in danger of succumbing to irreversible testosterone poisoning, he slowed his movements. He gave the sword a couple of lazy swings, then brought the blade to rest.

"This *is* the schedule," he said. "Swords, axes, daggers. We train until the Hersir decides we're ready for a trial."

I was speechless—and disappointed. "That's it? Just weapons in a field all day?"

"Beheading is the only way to kill a Mythical. Don't you think we should know what we're doing?"

"Yes." I tried to keep the irritation out of my tone. "I just thought there would be more"—I groped for a word—"*something*. Most Mythicals use magic. I assumed we'd learn how to defend ourselves from it." Rage magic was all well and good, but it did one thing: kill.

There was other kinds of magic in the world—power that could bend a person's will. Some things were worse than death.

Ulfar's smile didn't reach his eyes. "Most of us aren't half-breeds. It's dangerous to play with magic you can't control."

I swallowed. Was that a dig?

"You should warm up," he said. He jerked his chin toward a spot over my shoulder. "Weapons are over there."

I turned. A rack of broadswords stood on the edge of the field, various hilts poking out of the openings. I walked to the rack and stared at the blades. "Should I just...pick one?"

"Yes," a woman said behind me.

I spun. Maya and several others approached, their footsteps nearly silent on the soft grass. They moved with an eerie grace, almost like dancers. Each one carried a sword, the blades catching the rays of the sun just starting to spill across the field. When they reached me, they fanned out in an arrow formation. There were eight men and two women, including Maya.

Her purple eyes were even more mesmerizing up close. She planted the tip of her sword in the grass and looked pointedly between me and the sword rack. "Ready when you are."

Heat entered my cheeks as I faced the rack once more. The stares of the others bored into my shoulders. Why did they already have swords? Did they bring one from home? I let my hand hover over the weapons. The hilts were all different. Some were wrapped in basic leather, while others had metal grips. Undoubtedly, some blades were heavier than others. That wasn't always a bad thing. A lightweight sword was faster, but it was also easier for an opponent to knock away.

Behind me, someone cleared their throat.

I grabbed a longsword with a plain leather grip. As I pulled it free, it caught on the edge of the rack, making the other swords rattle and clack against one another. The heat in my cheeks turned to fire, and I clenched my jaw as I steadied the swaying rack with my free hand. When it stopped moving, I disentangled my sword from the others. Then I took a deep breath and turned around.

Maya held my gaze a moment before raising her voice. "All right. Positions, everyone."

The *drengir* jogged to the middle of the field. As if by some unspoken agreement, they split into two rows and paired off, one drengr facing another.

"Ready," Maya called.

As one, they sank into a sparring position—swords raised, legs in a slight lunge.

Maya looked at Ulfar, who still lingered on the side of the field. He nodded and ran to the center, where he faced the other female and fell into the ready position.

A horrible suspicion crept over me. With Ulfar on the field, that left just Maya and—

"You and I will partner off," she told me.

My stomach clenched. Had she planned this? Although, maybe I was just being paranoid. She was a Proven. Maybe she was supposed to assess my skill level.

She pulled her sword from the grass, flicked dirt off the tip, and stalked toward the field.

I stared after her for a moment, then followed.

She walked down the line of drengir. "Remember, this is sparring only. No power allowed."

Relief swept me. This was just regular sword training, then. I didn't have to worry about keeping my rage from spiraling out of control.

We reached the end of the line and faced each other. Her movements graceful, she sank onto her back foot and brought her sword up.

I did the same. My old swordmaster's voice echoed through my head. *Feet apart. Weight on the balls of your feet. Chin up, but not too far up. Breathe normally. Watch your oppo-*

nent's face, not their hands.

Maya's face was stern, her eyes two narrow, purple slits. Her features were delicate, her skin clear and glowing. The sun reflected off her blade, shining along the dull edge.

At least the swords were blunted. They wouldn't break the skin, but they could still inflict damage.

"Berserkers, ready!" Maya called.

As one, the drengir let out a deep, militaristic grunt.

I gripped my sword's hilt more tightly, the metal guard brushing my knuckles.

"Engage!" Maya lunged toward me, her sword arcing toward my neck.

My arms moved before my brain registered what happened. I whipped my blade up and to the side, blocking her blow. Metal clanged, and vibrations rattled down my arms.

She shoved off, quickly stepping back.

Smart. She didn't dance or bounce on her feet. She kept her boots flat on the ground, her blade angled in front of her body once more. The bob and weave might work great for boxing, but it was a terrible strategy in a sword fight. A good swordsman moved as little as possible, conserving his energy and maintaining his balance.

Around us, the other pairs fought. Clangs rang out, followed by grunts and the occasional shout.

It was all a distant blur. I couldn't afford to pay any attention to the others. I faced straight ahead, my eyes on Maya.

She came at me again, her black hair flying.

I stepped forward to parry—

—and caught only air.

She spun behind me and struck my lower back hard with the flat of her blade.

The force of the blow shoved me forward. Fire streaked up my spine. I stumbled and fell to one knee, one palm striking the ground. A moment later, cold steel touched my nape.

"Dead," Maya said above me.

Anger shot through my veins. I flung a hand back, knocking her blade away as I surged to my feet.

She tilted her head. "You want more?"

Ignoring the throbbing in my back, I fell into a ready lunge.

Something flashed in her eyes. It wasn't triumph. More like nasty anticipation.

The others continued sparring around us, but their matches were different than what just happened between Maya and me. They worked in a methodical rhythm, clearly running through drills designed to improve skill and hone muscle memory. They weren't trying to maim.

Maya stationed herself opposite me. She waited a second, then came at me, blade raised high.

I stumbled back, nearly tripping in my surprise.

Her shoulders bunched.

I swung my blade up, anticipating a downward strike.

She feinted, then went low. Her blade struck my upper thigh.

Pain blasted my quad. I sidestepped, lifting my sword so I could strike before she recovered.

In a blur, she ducked under my sword, spun, and came up swinging.

Our blades clashed. Metal screamed against metal. The muscles in my upper arms trembled. I clenched my teeth. Somewhere, in the dim parts of my consciousness, I became aware the fighting around us had stopped.

Maya jerked her arms back, abruptly removing the weight of her sword against mine.

Already leaning, I couldn't counter. My momentum carried me forward.

She tripped me as I stumbled past her. The ground reared up, and I landed hard. Again, steel touched my neck.

"Dead."

My back was on fire. My leg shook, the muscle spasming. Sweat dripped from my forehead and ran down my back. My ponytail dangled over my shoulder, the pale end touching the grass.

Maya leaned down, her voice low and even. "You don't belong here. Daddy might have bought your way in, but his money can't save you."

Her words slid into my mind like poison, soaking into the little hollows of anxiety and self-doubt.

"Save yourself some embarrassment and run back to the forest. Or seduce some rich man like your slut of a mother."

It was as if she'd lit a match and tossed it on the pool of anger simmering in my gut. Rage whooshed through me, spinning into a tight, seething ball. It settled in my chest, its pulsing energy like a heartbeat. In one motion, I snatched a handful of dirt, shot to my feet, and tossed it in her eyes.

She clapped a hand to her face and staggered back.

Lightning forked across the sky. Thunder boomed, and the smell of ozone filled the air.

Someone was shouting. I struggled to turn my head toward the source, but my muscles were locked.

My hand gripping the sword heated up. The ball in my chest spiraled into itself, gathering power. All the little hairs on my body lifted.

"Grab her sword!"

Ulfar. In some corner of my mind, an alarm sounded. If he tried to knock the weapon from my hand, the bundle of power inside me could burst from my body in an uncontrolled wave and kill him.

Or me.

Energy coursed through my veins, making my bones ache and my mouth water. Power sizzled halfway down my sword arm, then stopped—as if it encountered a barrier.

Lightning struck the far side of the field. A second later, thunder split the air. The smell of ozone thickened.

I had to let go of the sword. Even as I thought it, the power in my arm stretched toward my palm in a desperate bid to break free. The metal in my hand heated, and the scent of burning flesh filled my nose. A scream built in my throat. My vision blurred.

Light flashed. Thunder boomed so loud my ears rang.

Shadows moved in the edges of my vision.

A deep voice cut through the chaos. "Everyone step back."

There were gasps, followed by the shuffling of feet. One of the shadows moved toward me. It grew larger, then formed into the tall outline of a man who strode up and, without a moment's hesitation, *plucked* the sword from my hand.

The power in my chest snapped—the loss so abrupt I stumbled backwards and fell on my ass with a grunt.

Fortunately, everyone was too busy watching the newcomer to notice. In his hand, the sword glowed an eerie blue. Every few seconds, tiny currents of lightning licked around the blade and disappeared. He held the weapon away from his body, as if he was studying it. A brown cloak covered his head, obscuring his features. The garment had seen better days. Dark stains marred the front, and the tattered hem was splattered with mud.

I strained to see under the hood. To get a better glimpse of his features.

How had he taken the blade, and seemingly with no consequences? There was a reason berserkers always worked with a weapon. Raw magic—especially the kind borne of rage—was too much for the body to absorb. The energy needed a place to

go. Most berserkers preferred steel, which conducted electricity with no problem.

Skin, however, did not. It was one thing to channel rage
into metal, quite another to grab a charged weapon with bare
hands. The rules of magic dictated he should be writhing on
the ground, if not dead.

But he stood whole and unharmed, his head bent as he
looked over the sword like a man browsing the sporting goods
section in a department store. His shoulders rose and fell as if
he released a sigh. He gave the blade a small flick.

The power snuffed out.

As if it had never been.

He lifted his head and met my gaze.

I sucked in a breath.

His eyes were silver. The power swirled *there* now, in irises
forked with miniature lightning. He walked toward me, his
cloak floating out from his body.

Instinct urged me to scoot backwards, but I couldn't move.
Could hardly breathe.

Even with the hood covering his head, I should have been
able to make out most of his face. But every time I tried to get
a better look, it was as if his features shifted. The best I got
were glimpses—moments of clarity in which I could see his
forehead or nose. As he neared, his irises cleared, the lightning flickering out. His long shadow fell over me, his body
blocking the light from the rising sun. The strange, shifting
pattern continued, making it impossible for me to tell if he
was young or old, ugly or handsome. The only features I could
be certain of were those penetrating eyes and a dark blond
beard.

Norseman.

Viking.

Berserker.

He could have been any of those things. Somehow, even without anyone telling me, I knew he was all of them.

"Elin Berregaard?"

My throat was so dry, I had to swallow a couple times before I could speak. "Yes."

"Come with me." Sword still in hand, he turned on his heel and strode away, the tattered brown cloak fluttering behind him.

My stomach dropped as I realized I'd known who he was the moment he took my sword.

His clothes didn't matter.

I'd just met the Hersir of Bjørneskalle. The warrior who oversaw the Holmgang. The man who dictated whether I lived or died.

And he wanted to speak with me in private.

CHAPTER

FIVE

My heart pounded as I followed the Hersir into the castle. He stayed several paces in front of me, his long strides eating up the flagstones. I couldn't say I minded. It was easier to look at his cloak than those silvery eyes.

Ahead, the twin Norsemen loomed.

My heart beat faster.

The Hersir stopped at the statues' feet.

I stopped too, uncertainty fluttering in my chest like a trapped bird. After a moment, I moved to the Hersir's side. His cloak still obscured his face, and he stood so still he might have been another statue. He'd seemed tall when he loomed over me on the practice field. Now, I realized he was even taller than he'd appeared. At five-eleven, I was hardly small. But the way he towered above me, he had to be at least six foot five.

A groaning sound filled the air, and the Norseman on the right inclined its head. The statue pinned me with a stare, its eyes an otherworldly blue. "Elin-who-calls-herself-Haralds-dóttir," it said, its voice like rocks grinding against each other.

Its lips didn't move, but the blue brightened and dimmed as it spoke.

It seemed to be waiting for me to acknowledge it, so I cleared my throat. "Yes. That's me."

The blue flickered. "Are you worthy to enter?"

Was that a trick question? I chewed the inside of my cheek, wondering if it meant worthy in general or just worthy of using the stairs. Although, after what just happened outside, even the stairs were questionable. "Probably not."

The blue eyes gleamed, and the statue seemed to peer at me from its perch on the pillar, as if it was taking my measure. Just when I thought it was going to hoist its sword and take a swing at my neck, it straightened and settled back into place. "You may pass."

I released a breath I hadn't realized I was holding.

The Hersir turned to me, his features completely visible for the first time.

Then he *winked*.

I felt my eyes go wide.

He swept an arm toward the stone steps. "Shall we?"

Mind reeling, I preceded him through the arch and let him lead me up the spiral staircase that hugged the tower wall. Had he really just winked at me? And why did he suddenly look *a lot* younger than I thought?

I spent so much time turning these questions over and over in my mind, I didn't realize we'd reached the top of the tower until he stopped at a scarred wooden door. He tucked my sword under his arm and withdrew a skeleton key from his pocket. Just before he put it in the lock, he looked at me over his shoulder. "Sorry about the mess. I've been away for a while."

"Oh." I waved a hand. "Don't worry about it." Was I hallucinating? Maybe I'd hit my head when Maya tripped me, and I was dreaming this entire encounter. Because instead of condemning me to an immediate death, the Hersir just apologized for his *messy office*.

He opened the door and stood back, gesturing me inside.

I brushed past him and caught my breath. Wooden bookcases curved around the circular room from the floor to the ceiling. Books filled every shelf. Sunlight from a huge window spilled over the spines, making the gold lettering shimmer. There had to be thousands of volumes—each one bound in brightly colored leather decorated with runes.

"Sagas of the warriors," the Hersir said beside me. He rested the tip of my sword on the floor in front of him, his hands atop the pommel. "Every time a berserker does something notable, it—"

"Gets written down in the sagas," I said. "My father made me read these books. Only the most remarkable warriors get included." Harald had made it clear I wouldn't be one of them.

"Warriors and assassins," the Hersir said. He ran his gaze over the bookshelves. "What a noble bunch we are."

I looked at him sharply. He'd sounded almost...disapproving.

He strode to a huge desk flanked by two chairs. He placed my sword on the surface, which was scattered with scrolls and loose papers. Then he rounded the corner, removing his cloak as he went.

Surprise flared in my mind. His shoulders were so wide he probably had to angle sideways to fit through the castle's door frames. A plain black T-shirt stretched across his chest like it had been tailored to his dimensions. His only weapon was a black dagger strapped to his thigh—unusual in the sense that he wore the shiny obsidian weapon without a sheath. His pants were black leather—and they, too, looked custom made to hug his long legs and muscular ass—

I jerked my gaze up.

He balled the cloak in one large fist and tossed it on one of the chairs. There was no vagueness about his face now. Every feature was in sharp, clear focus. His forehead was high, with a subtle widow's peak. His hair was a shade or two lighter than his beard, the dirty blond brushed back and secured in a knot on the back of his head. While thick, his beard didn't hide his strong jaw and full lips, nor the cheekbones that would make any makeup artist swoon.

And he wasn't old. Same as I couldn't explain how I knew I was aging, I couldn't say why I knew he was young. Maybe it was his energy, which seemed to flow off him in waves. Even his eyes were youthful, which meant he wasn't the wizened immortal I'd imagined. The irises were no longer the eerie silver of the practice field. Now, they were a deep blue with faint laugh lines at the corners.

And I was staring into them.

With my mouth hanging open like a stray dog that just discovered a juicy steak.

I snapped my jaw shut and dropped my gaze to his chest. *Mistake.* It was just as impressive as the rest of him. His T-shirt clung to his pecs and hinted at washboard abs. The short sleeves hugged tan, rounded biceps streaked with...

I looked up and found him staring at me. "Is that blood?"

He blinked. Then he seemed to rouse himself before glancing at his arm. "Ah, probably. Yeah." He rummaged through the papers on his messy desk, lifting scrolls and moving books. After a second, he pulled a small package from the pile and held it aloft. "Baby wipes."

The surreal fog I'd been floating in for the past twenty minutes thickened as I watched him withdraw a towelette and swipe at his bicep. As he bent to his task, a lock of hair escaped the knot on his head and tangled in his beard. His leather pants rode low on his hips, the laces peeking from his waistband. His sandy brows pulled together, and the tip of his tongue poked between his lips.

Heat flooded my cheeks...and ventured other places.

"Have a seat," he murmured without looking up. "I'll just be a minute."

I tore my gaze off his mouth. What was I doing, ogling him like this? Out of nowhere, Maya's voice filled my head. *"Save yourself some embarrassment and run back to the forest. Or seduce some rich man like your slut of a mother."*

My blood ran cold as I sat in the open chair in front of his desk. I should be terrified of this man. He held my life in his hands. But instead of wondering if he planned on executing me, I was cataloging his most impressive physical traits like some kind of lovestruck teenager.

Or a nymph.

He finished with the wipes and settled behind his desk, where he studied me for so long I fought the urge to squirm. At last, he rumbled, "So Harald Berregaard sent his only daughter to Bjørneskalle."

I folded my hands in my lap. "Yes."

"And are you happy to be here?"

I hesitated. If I said no, I would seem ungrateful. But he might sense the lie if I said yes. He'd absorbed raw magic without batting an eye. What else was he capable of?

"It was either this or law school," I said.

He smiled, his teeth white and even in his beard.

I stopped breathing for a moment. Berserkers didn't smile. But this one did, and it was doing weird, fluttery things to my stomach.

"Maya bested you out there," he said.

The fluttery feeling faded. "You could say that."

He gestured toward the sword on his desk. "Well, for starters, you used the wrong weapon."

"How so?" The blade was like any other I'd used over the years.

"It's too long, for one thing." He ran his gaze down my torso. "How tall are you, about five-eleven?"

The heat I'd tried to banish came roaring back. "Yes. Exactly."

"This sword is better suited to someone with my reach. Even at my height, I probably would have chosen something shorter." His gaze shifted to a spot over my shoulder, and his voice turned thoughtful. "Even better..." He stood and rounded the desk with a purposeful look in his eyes.

Curiosity—and other emotions I wasn't going to think about—had me swiveling to watch him.

He went to a weapons rack mounted beside the door. An array of swords and daggers winked in the sun, but he passed them over in favor of a wooden bo staff, which he took down and carried back to his desk. He sat with the staff balanced across his knees, one hand resting on the dark-stained wood. "Maya was wrong to trip you, but it's bad form to throw dirt in an opponent's eyes."

"She called my mother a slut," I said flatly.

He appeared to mull that over. "She has good reason to hate the Fae. They killed her parents." He lowered his voice. "Ate them, actually."

That was horrifying—and something that rarely happened anymore. Only the high Fae preyed on humans, and most of them had stopped in recent centuries. Not because of any altruistic tendencies. Many would continue the practice if they could. But eating people tended to attract attention from human law enforcement, and no one wanted the scrutiny.

Still, what happened to her parents had nothing to do with me. "Not all Fae are like that," I said.

Amusement glimmered in his gaze. "I'm aware. I'm a half-breed myself."

I stared. *He* was Fae? The Hersir of Bjørneskalle wasn't even a pureblooded berserker?

"That surprises you," he murmured, the amusement lingering in his eyes.

"I... Yes." A dozen questions sprang into my mind. I'd been greeted with nothing but hostility since I arrived at the castle. How did he oversee the Holmgang when its participants reviled half his ancestry? Although, he hadn't said what kind of Fae he was. It wasn't always easy to tell, especially with half-breeds. He could be anything, his true form hidden behind glamour.

Into my stunned silence, he said, "Your mother was a nymph."

"That's right." I heard the defensiveness in my voice.

He stroked a big palm over the bo staff. "That's wild magic, the power of the Hunt."

He meant the Wild Hunt, an ancient practice in Faerie. Fiona said the high Fae started it as a way of whipping up devotion among their followers. True believers created an unpredictable but intense kind of magic, and the high Fae gobbled it up.

I shook my head. "My mother's magic was powerful, but I didn't inherit it."

"I wouldn't be so sure about that. Like a lot of wild things, Fae magic tends to fight when you try to control it. Pair that with a berserker's rage and you can end up with explosive results."

Explosive was a good way to describe my rage. It was like a firehose with no one manning the taps—powerful but ultimately useless because I couldn't direct it where it needed to go. Worse, I had no way to turn it off once it showed up.

And it rarely showed up when I needed it. As it had in the courtyard, it tended to only appear at the most inconvenient moments.

"I have a hunch, Elin."

The way he said my name sent sparks rushing over my skin. "Yes?"

"I think you're more powerful than you realize. You just need someone to train you."

"I've had a lot of tutors."

"And they taught you to use a sword?"

"Yes." From the time I was strong enough to lift one.

He stood, staff in hand. "It's as I thought. You've been using the wrong weapon."

It felt wrong to sit when he was standing, so I rose as I gestured to the staff. "You think I should use that?" I'd be scorned even more than I already was. The staff looked more like a walking stick than a weapon. Polished but plain, it barely reached his shoulder. He might as well have been holding a broom handle.

He seemed to read my thoughts, because he smiled. "The deadliest weapon is often one your opponent underestimates." Without warning, he tossed the staff across the desk.

My body moved before I had a chance to think. I snatched the staff out of the air, my palm smacking against the wood. At the impact, pain flashed through my hand, making me wince.

"What is it?" The Hersir circled the desk, concern in his eyes.

"Nothing." I'd caught the staff with my sword hand, which had blistered when I couldn't channel my rage. Distracted by the trip upstairs and our conversation, I'd forgotten all about it.

He drew close, his big body dwarfing mine. He took the staff from me and leaned it against his desk. Then he held out an expectant hand. "Let's see."

I curled my fingers over my palm and tucked my hand against my side. "I'm fine."

"It wasn't a request." His voice was soft, but the command was unmistakable.

Even so, it was nothing like the orders Harald gave. Maybe it had something to do with the way the Hersir gazed at me, a hint of a smile in his blue eyes. He was so close, I could feel his body heat.

"It's from the sword," I said, my voice husky in my ears as I placed my hand in his.

He bent his head and looked over the red weals on my palm. "I can fix this." He looked up. "May I?"

"A gift of yours?" Some Fae had that power.

He smiled. "I dabble."

His eyes really were the most incredible shade of blue. Like the sky where the horizon meets the ocean. "All right."

He turned my hand over and folded it between both of his. Then he closed his eyes and inhaled a slow, even breath. He smelled of clean sweat and wind—as if he'd just come from spending a long time outdoors.

My heart rate picked up.

"Don't be nervous," he murmured, his eyes still closed. "I've only killed one person during a healing." He squinted an eye open. "Just kidding."

I swallowed against a suddenly dry throat. First he apologized for his untidy office. Now he teased me. In no way had this meeting gone the way I anticipated.

Warmth suffused my hand, but it wasn't the kind of heat I'd felt when power had flowed through the sword. This was like sinking into a bubble bath. A faint tickling sensation scattered across my skin, traveling up my wrist to my forearm. There was a joy about it, something merry and uninhibited.

Fae magic. The realization made my lips part. Deep within me, something lifted its head. The heady, abandoned power that resided in me recognized the same power in him.

With his eyes closed, I was free to study his face, and I took in his proud nose and sensual lips. His bold brows and long, silky eyelashes. He was a beautiful man.

And I had no business noticing it.

A final pulse of heat flared across my palm. Then he opened his eyes. "There," he said softly. He held my hand a moment longer than necessary, his gaze mingling with mine before he released me.

I examined my palm so he wouldn't see how flustered I was. The angry red marks were gone, the skin smooth. I looked up and blurted, "What kind of Fae are you?" Immediately, I cringed inside. It was rude to ask. Not every Fae was "out" and some chose to cloak their appearance with glamour, especially if their true form fell on the hideous side. He could be a *sluagh* for all I knew—though I doubted it.

A teasing smile touched his lips. "Ah, if I told you that, you'd stop being curious about me."

My cheeks heated. Did he want me to be curious about him?

He grabbed the staff and held it out. "We start training tomorrow."

I stared dumbly. "We... Like you and me?"

"You and me." His gaze was steady.

A faint twang of discomfort hummed through me. Why was he singling me out?

As if he sensed my unease, he balanced the staff on both palms. "I believe you have it in you to be a great berserker. But you can't hide who you are, Elin. You're different than the others. Your power is different. If you train like you're ordinary, you'll waste your potential." He sobered. "Failure isn't an option at Bjørneskalle."

My hesitation vanished. My whole life, my two halves had battled each other. I'd tried throttling my magic so I could harness my rage. But he was saying I didn't need to. That I could use my magic and my rage together—and he'd teach me how.

I'd be a fool not to seize the opportunity.

I took the staff from his hands. Immediately, the rustle of leaves filled my ears, and a sense of well-being flowed through me like a cool river. The staff felt *right* in my hand, as if the wood wanted to be there. When I lifted my gaze, the Hersir was smiling.

"Tomorrow then," he said softly. "Meet me at the base of the Dragon Tower at noon."

"Okay. Thank you... My lord," I tacked on hastily.

He smile turned rueful. "That's a title I'll never have, Elin. The Rage Lords are unlikely to welcome one like me among their ranks. My given name is Hauk Sigridsson. Call me Hauk."

His voice slid around me like smoke. The air shifted, and I became aware of two things.

He stood close enough to kiss.

And he was staring at my mouth.

I waited, unmoving, the heat in me blooming anew. Growing hotter.

Dangerous.

He held my gaze a few more beats. Then he stepped back, breaking the spell. He moved behind his desk once more. "Get a good night's rest. I won't take it easy on you."

It was an obvious dismissal—and so abrupt I stood there for a second wondering if I'd imagined the interest simmering in his eyes, or the way his head had dipped ever so slightly toward mine.

But I was used to being dismissed. My reflexes kicked in, and I pivoted and went to the door. Just before I walked through, a dark thought popped into my head. I faced him, my throat like a desert. "Maya and the others..."

"Yes?"

"They might think... If you train me alone..." My face flamed. This was too awkward—especially after what just happened.

"You're worried they'll think you're getting special treatment for a reason."

"Yes." I stared at a spot on the floor, wondering if it might open up and swallow me.

"I understand your concerns," he said, and his tone was so reasonable I brought my head up. "Let's do this: I'll go to the tower early and wait on the roof. You follow later. That way no one will see us together."

"Won't they wonder why I'm not on the practice field?"

"I'll tell them you're training elsewhere, and they'll accept it." He smiled, and this time it held an edge. "I'm the Hersir of Bjørneskalle. I don't just swing the sword of justice, Elin, I swing it every time a drengr fails the Holmgang. And I'm the only one who decides who fails."

For a heartbeat—just a fraction of a second—his eyes fired silver. It happened so fast I couldn't be certain I'd seen it. Then he sat and pulled a sheaf of papers toward him. "I'll see you at the tower."

"Yes...Hauk." I left, and my heart didn't stop racing until I was in my room with my back pressed against the door, wondering what the hell I'd just gotten myself into.

CHAPTER
SIX

Prevailing wisdom said that every problem seemed better in the morning.

That was not the case the morning after my meeting with Hauk.

I'd spent the night upright in bed, my back propped against the lumpy pillow as I tried to figure out why he'd taken an interest in me. The obvious answer was that we were both half-breeds.

But I hadn't imagined the look in his eyes as he'd healed my hand—or the way he'd held it just a bit too long afterward. Did he assume I was open to advances because I was half nymph?

If I was smart, I'd march to his office and tell him I was going to train with the other drengr. That I intended to prove myself without extra help or secret rooftop meetings.

But as much as I hated to admit it, I needed him. He'd absorbed the full force of my rage as casually as someone picking up a cup of coffee. He was the only person at Bjørneskalle who could teach me what I was desperate to learn. As dawn light had crept through the window, I resolved to take what I could from him. Whatever his reasons for helping me, he was my best chance of getting through the Holmgang.

So I'd show up, train, and leave—and I'd keep my eyes and inappropriate thoughts to myself. Hauk Sigridsson was a means to an end. The sooner I got through his training sessions, the better.

Which was why I now found myself climbing the Dragon Tower's steps just before noon. The inside of the tower was a hollow ruin, its interior floors long gone. The spiral staircase was all that remained. Narrow and blackened with age, it soared up the tower's inner wall like the spine of some ancient beast.

As I ascended, I gave the staff in my hand a wary look. I'd placed it across my desk before settling on the bed last night. But I must have dozed off at some point, and when I woke the staff was tucked beside me.

My first thought had been that someone was playing a prank. But it was hard to imagine Ulfar or Maya sneaking into my room just to move a bo staff around. I'd tried gripping the smooth wood in my hands and looking into its past the same way I could sometimes read a door or piece of furniture. Like all living things, trees could communicate when they wanted to—even after they'd fallen or been cut down.

But the staff was silent. More than that, I got the sense it withheld information on purpose, like a stubborn toddler with its mouth clamped shut.

"You hear that?" I murmured to it now, my voice breathless from the effort of climbing. I didn't know if it could read my mind, so I spoke aloud just in case. "I think you're being childish. It's also rude to get in bed with women without asking."

Nothing. Not even a hint of a breeze or rustle of leaves. The smooth hickory stayed warm and quiet in my hand.

"Fine," I muttered. "Be that way."

I climbed a few more minutes, taking care not to look down. The staircase lacked a handrail and the treads were barely wide enough for one person. A single misstep could send me plunging to the bottom. It was almost enough to make me long for the flat ground of the practice field. Sweat dampened my temples and trickled down my back under the inflexible leather of my jerkin. If I made it through the Holmgang, it was going to be nothing but cotton for the rest of my immortal life.

As I neared the top, bright sunlight spilled down the steps. The roof was open in places, its wood rotted away. A rickety-looking ladder led to a square opening that revealed blue sky streaked with wispy clouds. I gritted my teeth and started up the rungs.

The ladder creaked ominously, the wood bowing under my weight. My heart pounded. My palm gripping the staff grew sweaty.

A hand appeared and Hauk's deep voice drifted down. "Need help?"

Relief washed over me. "Yes. Here." I hoisted the staff.

He took it. Seconds later, he gripped my hand and hauled me through the opening like I weighed nothing. He set me down on the roof and put his hands on my shoulders to steady me.

"Gotcha," he said softly, his eyes as blue as the sky behind his head.

Once again, his scent teased my nose, only this time it was a mix of leather and oak and something else—something dark and spicy that curled in my lungs and made me want to lean closer for more.

And that was just as hazardous as climbing the tower.

"Thanks," I said, taking a quick step back. The roof looked even more treacherous up here, its boards buckled and worn. In several places, big gaps showed the tower's flagstone floor two hundred feet below. My stomach pitched. "That's got to be a building code violation," I muttered.

He grinned. "Probably. But it stops people from coming up here. And you can't beat the view." He swept an arm toward the battlements.

I was too short to see over the stone, so I moved past him, picking my way over the creaking boards. The horizon came into view and I caught my breath. It was like I stood on top of the world. The cliffs of the fjord stretched toward the sky like jagged black teeth. Below, the fjord itself wound away from the castle like a dark blue ribbon. The colors were so vivid they didn't seem real. "It's beautiful," I murmured.

"Yes, it is," Hauk said at my side, and when I looked at him he was watching me.

My heart skipped a beat. *Show up, train, and leave.* That was what I'd decided. But as my pulse raced and sparks rushed over my skin, I had a hard time remembering why.

He held my gaze for a brief, shivering moment. Then he turned and strode down the battlements, stopping next to a backpack I hadn't noticed. My staff lay on the ground next to it. "Are you hungry?" he asked over his shoulder as he squatted in front of the pack.

"I..." Right on cue, my stomach growled.

He returned with a white takeout container and a bottle of wine. "It's not much of a picnic. I forgot to bring a blanket." He grimaced. "Or wineglasses."

The rich scent of garlic drifted from the container, making my mouth water. "Whatever's in there, I'll take it. I still haven't found the castle's cafeteria." Asher's basket had gotten me through the night, but there had been nothing left for breakfast.

"That's by design," Hauk said. He placed the wine and takeout box on the ground, then sat and motioned for me to do the same. "The castle doesn't have a mess hall. The drengir find food wherever they can."

I eased to the ground. "You mean we're on our own for meals?"

"It's part of the Holmgang." He uncorked the wine bottle and set it between us. "There's no meal service when you're on a quest. You fend for yourself. The Rage Lords decided the Holmgang should be the same." He flipped open the takeout box, revealing two enormous slices of pizza. He picked one up and held it out, mischief dancing in his eyes. "But the Rage Lords aren't here."

I stared at the garlic-and-cheese paradise in his hand. Was this a trick? The Holmgang was a series of tests. Maybe he wanted to see if I was willing to break the rules.

"Elin."

I met his eyes. His expression was kind, as if he understood my dilemma. "It's okay," he said. He tipped his head to the side, and it made him seem ordinary. Less intimidating. "You *do* like pizza, right?"

"I love it."

"Good." He pushed the slice into my hand, lifted his own, and took a healthy bite. "I don't trust anyone who dislikes pizza," he said around it. He swallowed. "Fuck, that's good."

That surprised a laugh out of me. "Where did you get all this?" If the castle lacked a mess hell, it probably didn't have a pizzeria.

"I opened a portal."

I stared. "You opened a portal just to get pizza?" Even the

most powerful berserkers only used portals when absolutely necessary. The energy drain could last for days.

"No, I opened a portal to get *New York-style* pizza." He licked pizza sauce off his thumb. "You can argue all you want that Chicago-style is better, but you'll never convince me. It's a hill I will gladly die on."

His enthusiasm was charming—and infectious—and I relaxed enough to take a bite.

He gave me an approving smile and took another bite. We ate in companionable silence for a few minutes, the sun chasing the chill from the air. After he'd finished, he handed me the wine bottle. "I can't vouch for the vintage, but the bloke at the pizza place said it's decent."

"I'm sure it's fine." I lifted the bottle to my lips.

"Skol," he said softly.

I paused. He'd stretched one long, leather-clad leg in front of him. He'd bent the other, and he rested his elbow on his knee, his thick bicep straining his sleeve. His hair was tied in a half ponytail today, leaving the rest of the dark blond strands to fall around his shoulders.

"Skol," I replied, then took a drink and handed him the bottle.

He drank immediately, his lips touching the same spot as mine on the rim.

We passed the bottle back and forth, and the wine spread through my veins, chasing away my nerves and making me bold enough to ask, "You said *bloke*. And I hear London in your accent."

He wiped his mouth with the back of his hand. "Knightsbridge. I lived there while I attended university." His jaw tightened. "My father is Irish. My berserker half comes from my mother."

Of course, I thought. Sigrid was a woman's name...and he was Hauk *Sigridsson*.

"Your mom must be proud of you for becoming Hersir," I said.

He made a low sound of assent. "She is, but nothing I do can come close to her exploits. You've read the sagas. Have you heard of Sigi the Bold?"

Surprise tripped through me. "Your mother is Sigi the Bold? The berserker who defeated a Roman legion?"

"I wouldn't go that far. It was probably just a couple of cohorts."

"She's a *legend*," I insisted. "One of the best fighters in the sagas."

He gave a good-natured groan. "Please don't ever let her hear you say that. I'll never hear the end of it." He stood and extended a hand. "Come on. We carb loaded. Now it's time to train."

I let him pull me up. "What about the gaps in the boards?"

"What about them?" He grabbed my staff and went to the center of the roof. Feet braced apart, he twirled the staff hand over hand, spinning it like a windmill. His shoulders bunched and flexed as he worked, and it was a hell of a lot more impressive than Ulfar's demonstration the day before.

"I'd rather not fall *through* them," I said, skirting a gap as I walked forward. "I'm not immortal."

"Neither am I."

I stopped. "Of course you are. You're the Hersir."

He ceased his spinning. "There's no rule that says the Hersir has to be immortal."

"But..." Confusion swamped me. "The Hersir is the most powerful berserker in the Guild."

"I'm sure there are some, your father included, who would debate that. But I wouldn't lie to you, Elin. I'm as mortal as you are, so you can trust me that the roof is safe. We'll train away from the openings."

My brain refused to process what he was telling me. "I don't understand. Are you short a couple of kills?"

He shook his head, his face resigned. "I could fell an army and it would make no difference. I'm cursed, courtesy of my father." His lips twisted in a humorless smile. "He has a way of getting his point across."

His own father cursed him? "Why would he do such a thing?"

Hauk leaned on the staff, one hand draped over the top. "He was angry about me choosing a berserker's life. His blood is strong enough that I was born immortal. He pressured me to stay in Faerie, but I dislike the politics. His exact words were, 'If you insist on spending your days sucking Odin's dick, you don't deserve immortality.' When I told him that suited me just fine, he hit me with the curse. He stripped my immortality, but he also made it so I have to accept every quest I'm offered."

I swallowed a gasp. "You can't refuse?"

"The curse won't even let me say the words. If someone asks, I have to say yes."

Horror was like acid in my gut. As the Hersir, he likely received hundreds of petitions a year. Most Mythicals were immortal in the sense that they were immune from disease and aging, but they could be killed by beheading. Few were willing to risk their necks taking on a rogue immortal, so they asked the Rage Lords to send a berserker.

But every warrior in the Guild had the right to turn down a quest. They didn't even need a reason. Berregaard Manor saw a regular number of visitors who petitioned Harald to carry out a kill. Most left disappointed.

Hauk's father hadn't just cursed him. He'd made him a slave.

"Do you think he might change his mind?" I asked.

He released a short, bitter laugh. "Not a chance. My father thrives on cruelty. He kidnapped my mother and held her prisoner in Faerie until she agreed to wed him. Theirs wasn't a happy union. Half her blood runs in my veins, and he hates me for it."

Understanding bloomed within me, relief hot on its heels. He wasn't helping me because I was a nymph. He was doing it because he knew how it felt to be hated by someone who should love him without conditions.

That revelation made my voice husky. "It seems we have more in common than I thought."

He straightened. "I know how Harald treated your mother...and you. You've got two choices. You can let anger eat you alive, or you can use it." He considered the staff for a moment, his eyes running over the dark wood. Then he looked at me. "Which will it be?"

I held out my hand. "Show me how to use it."

"Good choice," he murmured. Then, as he'd done in his office, he tossed me the staff.

I snatched it from the air, and it seemed to *jump* into my palm—almost like a magnet.

"Sparring only," he said. "No rage, no magic." He shook out his arms like a boxer before a match. "Show me what you've got."

"You're not going to use a weapon?"

He tossed me a cocky smile. "I don't need one. I doubt you'll even land a blow."

I felt my eyebrows pull together.

He pointed. "Anger. Good. Use that." He danced back, gesturing for me to come at him. The boards under his feet creaked and groaned.

My heart pounded. *He'd better be right about this roof.*

He bounced on the balls of his feet. "I haven't got all day!"

I lifted the staff. He'd said sparring only—no magic or rage. That made things simpler.

Didn't it?

The sun beat down—uncharacteristically bright for November. The rays picked up the lighter streaks of blond in his hair. Mischief in his gaze, he grinned at me. "Scared?"

The staff warmed under my hand. A breeze caught at my hair, tossing white-blond strands around my face. From somewhere came the faint sound of wind rustling through leaves.

Was I afraid? "Hardly," I muttered, then sank into a crouch.

Anticipation—and something that might have been satisfaction—flashed in his eyes. "Bring it, shieldmaiden."

The staff vibrated against my palm. Surprise registered in my mind, but I pushed it aside. I'd unravel the staff's secrets later. Right now, I had an arrogant berserker to deal with.

I spun the staff in a slow circle and advanced forward.

Hauk bent his knees.

In a burst of speed, I darted forward, aiming for his shoulder.

He grabbed the staff, yanked me onto my toes, and shoved me backwards.

My boots skidded against the roof's uneven planks, and I stumbled back a few steps before regaining my balance. Heart racing, I glanced over my shoulder. The edge of the tower was a safe distance away.

"Sloppy," Hauk said. "Windmilling the staff might look good in action movies, but it burns too much energy. You'll wear yourself out before you start."

I sputtered. "You were just doing it!"

"Yeah, but I'm better than you."

My angry gasp echoed around the roof.

He crooked his finger. "Again."

I took a deep breath...then charged him, staff aimed high. At the last second, I slashed it down toward his thigh.

He jumped, clearing it. While I was off balance, he grabbed my shoulder, spun me around, and pinned my back against his chest, one meaty arm like a band across my shoulders. His hips aligned with my ass, and his rock-hard abs pressed against my spine.

The breath left my lungs.

He spoke into the hair near my temple. "Better. But stop going for big strikes. With someone my size, you need to focus on lots of little jabs. I'm big, but you can tire me out if you're patient."

His breath in my ear raised goosebumps on my skin. The staff heated under my hand. I pulled my elbow forward, then jerked it back and into his ribs.

He grunted, loosening his hold.

I slipped under his arm and whirled away. Facing him, I sank back into a crouch.

"Nice." Approval shone in his eyes. He clutched at his ribs a second, then shook his arms out to his sides. "Again."

We circled each other. I kept the staff angled in front of my body, my knees slightly bent.

He made a couple grabs at me.

I danced back.

He laughed and kept circling, his movements light and graceful. More sunlight poked through the clouds, big shafts of it spilling across the roof.

We continued circling. Sweat trickled down my back and dampened my temples. The wind caught at his hair, tugging strands from his ponytail. He shoved them back.

I rushed him. In a blur of movement, I flipped the staff, poked his arm, and quickly sprinted back.

"Yes! More like that."

We fell back into our positions, circling...circling. I had to wait for the right moment. Keep him off guard.

He grinned. Oh yeah, he knew what I was doing.

An answering grin pulled at my cheeks. I couldn't help it. Sparring had never been like this. Had never been fun...or arousing.

The staff hummed, and I sensed it was pleased—almost *proud*. I danced forward, intending to jab.

Hauk swatted the staff away.

I ducked, then struck his ankle. *Got him.*

He yelped and sidestepped. "Good one."

Emboldened, I jabbed again.

He swatted me back.

Again, jab.

He missed me.

Again, jab. Another hit, this time to his chest.

Half grunting, half laughing, he whirled away.

The move forced me to pursue. The battlements loomed behind him.

I darted a look over his shoulder. *Too close.* What if he fell?

He grabbed the staff with both hands and yanked me hard against his chest.

I jerked backwards, but it was like trying to move a mountain. The staff was trapped between our bodies. His heart thundered against mine. My breasts pressed against his chest.

"You lost concentration," he said, his voice breathless. He was so close I could see the striations in his irises. His eyelashes were dark and thick, his lips full and sensual.

Suddenly, it was hard to breathe. To think. I had to focus to get a response out. "I-I know. I was worried you'd fall."

There was nothing but the staff between us. His hips brushed mine, his body warming me from shoulder to thigh. "You worried about me," he murmured. "I like that."

My heart pounded, the beat traveling from my chest to the aching place between my legs.

His gaze searched mine. Loose strands of hair framed his face, catching in his beard.

"Elin." His voice was low and husky.

"Hersir..."

"Call me Hauk," he said, and lowered his mouth to mine.

CHAPTER
SEVEN

His kiss was gentle, but only for a second. The staff clattered to the ground as he took my face in his hands and pushed his tongue inside, stroking it boldly against mine. His big hands tangled in my hair, and his cock brushed the top of my sex, lighting a fire inside me. I gasped, and my indrawn breath was *him*—his scent and essence. He tasted like rain and power and electricity. Like grass and wind and magic. It flooded my lungs and joined the desire surging hot in my veins.

He tugged my hair, tipping my head back. Plunging in deep, hungry strokes that made my nipples ache and moisture pool between my thighs.

A moan wound its way up my throat. He was devouring me. Worshipping me with his kiss.

And I needed it everywhere.

He pulled back, his nostrils flaring. His chest heaved, and his eyes had shifted to silver. "I can smell your need," he growled. "How wet you're getting."

My sex clenched, lust urging me to grab his shirt and pull

him back. To beg him to transfer his kiss to the hot, needy pulse between my legs. "Please," I managed, my voice little more than a croak.

"Please, what?" he demanded, his gaze searing mine. His fingers bit into my upper arms. "Ask for what you need."

I was too turned on to be coy. "Please fuck me."

He growled and yanked me against him. "Can't resist you," he muttered before crushing his mouth to mine once more.

My head swam, and I didn't realize he'd lowered me to the ground until my back touched the roof. *No matter.* Nothing beneath me mattered. All I cared about was the big, powerful man on top of me, his beard tickling my skin as his mouth sucked at my neck. His clever hands unraveled the laces of my jerkin, and then his rough-skinned palm skimmed up my stomach and found one of my breasts. He stroked me over the satin of my bra, then yanked the cup down.

I moaned, thrusting my chest into his hand as electricity frazzled through me.

Face still buried in my neck, he played with my nipple, rolling and pinching the sensitive peak. He trailed kisses down my throat, then lifted his head, his hot gaze on my chest. "Oh, I need to see both of these beauties," he murmured, then tugged my entire bra down, bunching the cups under my breasts. The material pushed them together and made my nipples poke toward the sky. They tightened further under his rapt gaze, the pink points begging for attention.

"You are utter perfection," he rasped. He bent and suckled one nipple, then the other, his tongue teasing and flicking. Each pull of his mouth made me hotter and wetter, until I was whimpering with every breath, my need soaring to the point of pain.

He slid a knee between my thighs, and his fingers worked at the laces of my pants.

"Yes!" I cried. My spine bowed as I arched, eager for him to find the place I needed him to be. He fumbled with the laces, made a frustrated sound, and ripped them away in one quick, wrenching motion.

My sex spasmed, my hips rolling. My body delighted in his strength. Welcomed his power. I lifted my ass as he tugged my pants down, then moaned loudly when he jerked my panties aside.

He paused, his gaze on the heated flesh between my legs. "You're bare here," he rasped in a strangled voice. "I can see everything."

I lifted my hips wantonly, knowing what he must see. My clit throbbed so fiercely it had to be swollen past my folds. "Touch me," I begged.

With a pleasure-laced groan, he thrust his hand between my thighs, his fingers parting my slick lips and finding my clit.

I arched, pleasure exploding as he rubbed my pulsing center. I was so wet I could hear it as he circled the aching nub with his thumb.

"Fuck," he gasped, his voice ragged. "Such a soft, wet pussy. Hot and sweet." He rose above me, his silvery eyes narrowed to slits. He withdrew his hand from my sex.

I cried out with loss and tried to pull him back down.

"Easy, baby," he murmured. "I need a taste." Slowly and deliberately, he licked me from his fingers, and his eyes went molten. "Like candy on my tongue."

I lay there, shivering, as he sucked his fingers clean.

He held my stare as he untied his pants. "One day soon, I'm going to spread those long legs wide and lick your sugary cunt until you scream."

My breath caught, the filthy words sending fresh moisture rushing to my sex.

"But right now, I'm going to fuck you so hard you see stars."

A sharp *caw* split the air, the sound so loud my ears rang.

Hauk was on his feet in seconds, his body braced for battle. I scrambled to my knees, my head swimming from the abrupt cessation of pleasure.

A raven sat on the battlements, its ebony head cocked sideways as it pinned us with a beady glare. The bird was huge, its body the size of a dog's.

Hauk's shoulders relaxed. "Just a raven."

I shoved my clothes back into place and stood on unsteady legs.

The bird let out another ear-splitting *caw*. It hopped off the battlements and onto the roof.

"Shoo!" Hauk waved his hand.

The raven didn't move.

I stood, holding my ruined pants together with one hand. "Are its eyes supposed to be blue?"

Hauk answered without taking his gaze off the bird. "Not normally. The ravens at Bjørneskalle are different."

That was right, I thought, remembering what Harald had said in the car. I lowered my voice. "Does this mean someone died?"

"No. They never come alone like this."

As he spoke, the bird spread its wings, hopped into the air, and wheeled away from the tower. As we watched it fly off, the pleasure-fueled haze of the last ten minutes dissipated, leaving cold reality behind. I'd nearly had sex with a man I met yesterday. And not just any man—the Hersir of Bjørneskalle. The berserker who held my fate in his hands.

Well, I'd certainly fallen into them.

He faced me, his expression inscrutable. "Elin—"

"I should go," I said quickly. I looked around for the staff and spotted it on the ground. *Where it fell as we ate each other's faces off.* Cheeks flaming, I went to it.

Hauk got there first. He scooped it up but didn't hand it over. "Elin, wait." He stepped close, his voice a low, urgent rumble. "I won't say I regret what just happened, because I don't. I feel a connection with you. I believe you feel it too."

It would have been pointless to deny it, especially when my body still ached with it. My sex throbbed, my flesh hot and unfulfilled. My lips were swollen from his kiss, and from the way my neck was tingling, I was going to have a beard rash there by evening.

"You do, don't you." He made it a statement, his eyes flickering from blue to silver.

"Yes," I whispered.

He put the staff in my hand and wrapped my fingers around it. Then he pulled the gaping halves of my pants together and tucked them under my jerkin. He brushed his knuckles over my cheek, murmuring, "We don't have to figure it out right now. Just promise you'll come back here tomorrow."

"I..." And what would happen then? Was I prepared for the inevitable? Because even now, my nipples tightened at the thought of finishing what we'd started.

"Promise you'll come back. That's all I'm asking of you right now."

"All right."

Relief flashed across his features. "All right."

The wind picked up, bringing a chill that had been missing since morning. "I'll go first," I said. "It's best if we stay apart." Anyone seeing us together would immediately know what we'd been doing.

He nodded. "I'll wait a bit and then follow."

Staff in hand, I went to the ladder, and I didn't look back as

I scrambled down and walked quickly to the stairs. The descent was easier than the climb up had been. Or maybe I was just too stunned to worry about falling. I reached the bottom of the spiral and hurried toward the main keep, my emotions swirling so fast I couldn't catch hold of one long enough to decide how I felt.

The castle loomed over me. I walked faster, my head down as I passed a clump of shrubs that clung to the thick stone wall.

A shadow darted forward in my peripheral vision.

Then something struck me hard across the stomach.

Pain exploded in my ribs.

I collapsed, the staff flying from my hand.

CHAPTER

EIGHT

I fell to my hands and knees, wheezing.

Maya's voice dripped venom above me. "You fucking whore. I was right about you."

My eyes watered. Every inhale sent a knife plunging into my side. Bracing my weight on one palm, I probed my ribs with my fingertips, trying to tell if she'd broken them. If she'd struck me with a sword, I should be bleeding...or worse. The leather of my jerkin wasn't thick enough to stop a blade.

"Nothing to say?" Her boots moved into my line of sight. Close enough to kick me in the face.

Gritting my teeth, I grabbed the staff and stood. Fire streaked through my ribs, and I wanted nothing more than to hunch over, but I forced myself upright. My heart pumped in a furious rhythm, and my vision blurred as the knife in my ribs twisted deeper.

She stood in front of the tangle of shrubbery with a sword in her hand. Her amethyst eyes glittered with malice as she ran her gaze down my body in a sweep that made my skin crawl. "You walk in here with your big tits and bimbo curves and think you can fuck your way into the Guild. Do you have any idea what the rest of us have endured in this place? The endless drills and mock battles? The exhaustion? The *starvation*?"

My stomach clenched. Hauk had given me pizza...

"As soon as I heard the Rage Lords were permitting a nymph to attempt the Holmgang, I predicted you'd do your training on your back. I just didn't think you'd start so soon."

I dragged in a breath. "Get out of my way." I blinked hard, struggling to focus. I was no match for her, and this wasn't friendly sparring on the Dragon Tower. If she came at me, I'd lose.

"Or what? You'll hit me with your stick?" She flicked a dismissive glance at the staff. "I saw you leave with it today. It was obvious where you were going." She gave a short, scornful laugh. "Gods, he didn't even try to hide it. Men are pigs regardless of the species."

The staff vibrated once, hard. I tightened my grip so I wouldn't drop it. "You don't know what you're talking about."

She stepped closer. "I know *exactly* what I'm talking about."

Behind her, the shrubs shivered. I glanced at them, and they stopped.

Maya continued. "If you think he's helping you because you're Fae, think again. I don't care how many trips you make to the Dragon Tower, you'll never be good enough for him. You're not fit to kneel at his feet, although I'm sure you did plenty of that during your *training* session."

My thoughts whirled. Hauk *was* helping me because I was Fae. The same as him. And she hated the Fae, so why did she sound almost reverent when she spoke of him?

She must have seen the confusion on my face, because her lips curved in a slow smile. "You don't know, do you? He hasn't told you who he is."

My heart thumped harder, and a sense of doom settled over me. He'd never said what kind of Fae he was. And I hadn't pressed because I hadn't wanted to be rude.

The shrub moved again, the greenery scratching against the castle wall. Vines emerged from the leafy base and raced over the ground.

Death nettles. Vicious things. Their sting was agony. Too much of their venom could kill. Asher claimed they were just misunderstood.

Maya didn't seem to notice. "Do yourself a favor, nymph. The next time you spread your legs for the Hersir, ask him about his father. Because I can guarantee he'll never take you home to daddy."

The death nettles kept coming, the twisting vines rushing toward her feet.

"Maya," I said, "we really need to move." The plant was known to kill deer that wandered into its territory.

She continued as if she hadn't heard me. "Your kind isn't good enough for Sigridsson. He'll take what he wants and then he'll get sick of it, just like your father got his fill of your mother."

I moved without plan or thought. One moment I faced her, the next I had her pinned against the castle wall with the staff across her neck and my face an inch from hers.

"You do *not* talk about my mother," I snarled.

Wind whipped around us. The staff hummed under my hand. At the bottom edge of my vision, something glowed green.

Not something, I realized. *My fingers.* Tiny vines crept across my skin and twirled around my knuckles.

Maya's eyes widened, white showing around the purple. Her lips moved, but only a gurgle emerged.

"I don't care what you think of me," I said, "but keep your mouth shut about her. Understand?"

The scent of rain and roses filled my lungs. Maya's face turned red.

I pressed the staff harder against her throat. "Don't speak of her again."

Her eyelids drooped as she teetered on the edge of passing out.

I stepped back.

She slid to the ground in a heap.

The death nettles rushed in, parting around my feet like a river around a boulder. The vines moved swiftly, slithering over her limbs and crisscrossing her chest. They jerked as they stung over and over. Within seconds, hundreds of white welts pebbled her skin, the weals already weeping.

"Stop!" I cried.

The death nettles paused, and I *felt* their attention turn toward me. Their hiss was like water sizzling in a pan. *"She'ssss bad. Poisssson in her heart."*

My breath caught. Plants didn't speak with a human voice. Like trees, they communicated in feelings and images. But I'd heard the death nettles.

And they'd heard me. They waited now—listening.

"You're hurting her," I said.

The prickly leaves trembled. *"She'ssss bad,"* they repeated. *"Nassssty bersssserker."* The vines began to move.

"N-No!" I lifted the staff, braced for it to hum or leap with power.

Nothing happened. Its smooth wood was a broom handle once more.

The death nettles stretched over Maya's face, covering her features in a thicket of green.

Panic beat at me. They were killing her. I aimed the staff at the bush. "Friends! Please, I'm begging you to stop!"

They continued writhing and stinging. Maya's body was almost completely covered in green.

"ELIN!"

I swung around at Hauk's shout. He pounded toward me, his face pale.

"Hauk!" I rushed to meet him. "You have to help, I can't control—"

He sprinted past me. In a blur of movement, he scooped Maya's sword from the ground and aimed it at the death nettles. Blue fire streaked down the blade and blasted across the vines like spray from a blowtorch.

I stumbled back, squinting against the light.

Hauk swung the sword in a wide arc. The death nettles hissed and retreated.

Maya lay still on the ground. Her eyes were swollen shut, her skin oozing venom.

I watched helplessly as Hauk tossed the sword away and knelt beside her. He stripped the remaining vines from her body, then gripped the top of her jerkin and ripped it open, rending the leather like it was tissue paper. He lay his palms on her chest and bent his head.

I put a hand over my mouth. "Is she..." I couldn't bring myself to finish.

"She's not dead." He shot me a hard look over his shoulder. "Move back, I need to do something." He waited for me to obey, then bent his head once more. A second later, blue light pulsed from his hands.

Maya's chest jerked. She made a choking sound.

"That's it," Hauk murmured. He rolled her to her side and patted her back. She coughed and sucked in a few deep breaths. He brushed the hair back from her forehead and used his thumb to lift one of her swollen eyelids.

Rapid footsteps made me turn. Ulfar and three other drengir approached. When they caught sight of Maya, they broke into a run.

Hauk stood and put up a palm, halting them before they could touch her. "Just a brush with death nettles. Take her to her room. I'll stop by in a bit to check on her."

Ulfar looked at me.

"Ulfar," Hauk said, a hint of warning in his tone.

Accusations burned in Ulfar's eyes, but he swung his gaze back to Hauk. "Yes, Hersir?"

"Take Maya to her room."

Ulfar touched his fist to his chest and bowed stiffly. He and the other drengir lifted Maya, who moaned through swollen lips. The men spent a moment maneuvering, obviously trying not to hurt her, then seemed to realize there was no way around it. Each man took charge of a limb, and they started toward the castle.

Hauk and I stood silent as they moved down the wall, Maya's long black hair trailing like a banner. When they were out of earshot, he turned to me with a grim expression. "What happened?"

"She attacked me."

"That's not what it looked like, Elin."

My jaw dropped. "What? She was waiting for me. She struck me with her sword—" I sucked in a breath as I realized the pain in my ribs was gone. I pressed a hand to my side, but there was nothing, not even a twinge of discomfort.

"What is it?" he asked, frowning.

"I...don't know. She hit me, but I don't feel it now. I'm surprised the blade didn't slice the leather."

"The jerkins are enchanted. They're impervious to fire and tearing. It's why we wear them to train."

I lowered my hand. That explained why Maya's blow hadn't cut me, but it raised another question in my mind. "You ripped her jerkin in two just now." Effortlessly.

A muscle leapt in his jaw.

"What kind of Fae are you?" I asked.

He was so still, I didn't think he was going to answer. Then he muttered, "My father is one of the High Fae."

Not a lesser Fae. Not even a major Fae. His father was worlds apart—literally—from anything I was used to. I was the daughter of a species best known for throwing orgies.

He was the son of a god.

I spoke through numb lips. "Were you going to tell me?"

"Yes." He held my stare, his eyes back to that intense shade of blue. "And if you know anything about the High Fae, you know I can't lie."

No, but he could twist the truth until it was no longer recognizable. That was what the High Fae did. They manipulated and evaded. Exploited and charmed.

Had he charmed me on top of the Dragon Tower?

He stepped close. "Elin, listen—"

A chorus of *caws* filled the air, and a flock of ravens swooped toward us. There were dozens of them, each bird sleek and black as midnight. They wheeled in the sky, cawing loudly as they flew in a tight circular formation just above our heads.

They alert the Hersir when someone approaches the gate...or when a drengr dies.

I jerked my gaze to Hauk's. "Maya—"

"No," he said, his expression grim. "That's their formation for a visitor."

My heart began to pound, as if my body knew something my brain had yet to register.

"A specific kind of visitor," he rasped.

I looked at the birds. I didn't need him to finish.

I already knew.

"The Rage Lords are here."

CHAPTER
NINE

I sat on my bed with my head in my hands.

The Rage Lords were at Bjørneskalle.

Harald was a Rage Lord.

Was my own father about to sentence me to death?

"It won't come to that," Hauk had said as he walked me to my room. He'd stopped outside the door and cupped my face in his hands. "I'll talk to the lords, tell them Maya stumbled into the shrub."

I'd shaken my head. "They won't believe that. Didn't you see the way Ulfar looked at me? He thinks I set the death nettles on her."

"He's probably the one who notified the Rage Lords," Hauk growled. Then he stroked a thumb over my cheek. "Just sit tight and don't worry. I'm the Hersir here. I won't let anything happen to you."

That had been an hour ago. I'd followed his order to sit tight, but I was failing at the not worrying part. If everything was fine, wouldn't he be back by now? Ulfar had been present both times I lost control of my rage. If he told the lords what he'd seen, they might very well believe I attacked Maya.

The problem was, I wasn't entirely certain I *hadn't*.

I lifted my head and peered at my hand, looking for any sign of the tiny, creeping vines I'd seen when I pinned her to the wall, but there was nothing.

I hugged my knees to my chest. I'd probably imagined it, but I hadn't imagined the pain in my ribs after she hit me—or how it had vanished while I choked her with the staff.

I hadn't imagined the staff's power, either. I didn't know how it worked—and I definitely couldn't control it—but there was no denying it possessed *some* kind of energy. Hauk had taken it with him when he left in case the Rage Lords asked to see it. "Let them examine it all they want," he'd said. "They'll find it's just a well-polished piece of wood."

But I didn't believe that, and I hadn't missed his careful phrasing. He hadn't lied. The *Rage Lords* might decide the staff was harmless.

That didn't mean it wasn't.

Someone knocked on the door.

My heart rate sped up. I swung my legs over the side of the bed. "Yes?"

Ulfar walked in, unconcealed animosity on his face. "Let's go. You're wanted in the Hersir's office."

"Who wants me?"

His response was to turn around and walk out. He stopped in the hall outside the door.

Sighing, I stood—and tripped over the staff. Biting back a curse, I stared at it lying on the ground. I'd *seen* Hauk take it.

Yet here it was.

"What are you doing with that?" Ulfar demanded from the doorway. He charged inside.

I picked up the staff and straightened just as he reached me.

"What kind of trickery is this?" he asked. "The Hersir had that in his office. He was showing the Rage Lords."

I lifted my shoulders. "Apparently, it thinks I'm better company."

"You have a lot of nerve making jokes right now. The lords are here because of you."

"Really? I heard they assembled for their annual cock-measuring contest."

He sucked in a breath. Then his voice went low and cruel. "Laugh while you can. The Rage Lords will see you for what you are. The Hersir's whore—"

His words choked off as I pressed the tip of the staff against his throat. Where the rounded end had been there was now a metal spear with a wicked-looking point. Ulfar looked down at it, his face a mask of shock.

I leaned forward, and the spear pierced his skin. Not too much. Just enough to send blood trickling down his neck. "As I said, my friend here seems to prefer my company. So I suggest you go. I'll find my own way to the Hersir's Tower."

Ulfar made a soft sound.

"I'll take that as a yes."

He gave the merest hint of a nod.

"Go," I whispered.

He left so quickly the draft from his departure fluttered my hair.

I studied the staff, which still sported a spear tip. "Thanks."

The wood was silent.

I lay it on the bed and frowned at it. "Please stay here. If Lord Harald sees you, he'll turn you into firewood." I went to the door and looked over my shoulder. "I mean it. Don't follow me."

The staff lay on the rumbled bed, its polished wood unremarkable save for the spear at the end.

I started down the hall. The staff's mysteries would have to keep for the moment. I wasn't sure who waited for me in Hauk's office, but showing up late wouldn't help my case.

That thought was enough to make me walk faster, and I was flushed and breathless by the time I reached the statues at the bottom of the staircase leading to the Hersir's Tower.

The Norseman on the left rumbled, its eyes shining with blue light. "Elin, daughter of the wood. What mischief have you made today?"

How was I supposed to answer that? "It's…complicated."

The statue made an odd noise, like rocks tumbling over each other. If I hadn't known better, I might have thought it was laughing.

"You may pass," it said at last. "But remember, shield-maiden-who-walks-in-bough-and-bower, the raven watches."

Heat entered my cheeks as I remembered the large raven from the Dragon Tower. Was it connected to the statues somehow? I'd just threatened Ulfar with a teleporting bo staff. Anything was possible.

I cleared my throat. "I will."

The Norseman resumed its usual position. The blue light faded and disappeared.

Heart pounding, I passed between the statues and climbed the spiral staircase. When I reached the landing, Hauk's door was ajar.

And Harald was seated behind Hauk's desk, his platinum hair stark against his black leather coat.

He caught sight of me and stood, his gaze chilling me to the bone. "You took your time."

I entered, my heart thumping so hard I wondered if he could hear it.

A second man sat in one of the chairs facing the desk. As soon as I noticed him, he stood and turned around. He was tall, and his sword and dress identified him as a berserker. He wore his black hair long, half of it tied back from his face. He was handsome enough, with a square jaw and clear gray eyes. Black stubble covered his cheeks and chin. His gaze roamed over me.

My scalp prickled. He was a stranger, yet his face seemed familiar.

I looked at Harald. "Where is the Hersir?" He'd promised to protect me.

Harald spoke in a cold, flat voice. "Ulfar Gundersen says you lost control of your rage in training yesterday. And today you attacked another drengr—a Proven ready to take her place among the Guild."

"I didn't—"

"You've disgraced yourself and your house."

"I didn't attack her," I insisted. "She struck me and I—" I cut myself off before I could admit I'd choked Maya with the staff.

"Acted in self-defense?" he suggested. "That's what Sigridsson claims."

My heart swelled. "He's right." I stopped there. It seemed wise to say as little as possible, especially since I didn't know what Hauk had told him and the other lords.

Harald watched me, his expression dispassionate. "Sigridsson may have vouched for you, but the fact remains that you couldn't even last a day without losing control. And you and I both know what happened in the courtyard when you arrived."

My throat went dry. Was he pulling me from the Holm-gang? I glanced at the stranger, whose presence took on a new, ominous edge. He carried a berserker's sword. He could remove my head in a single blow.

"You can't remain at Bjørneskalle," Harald said.

My knees loosened. He was really going to do it. My own father was going to have me killed.

He moved around the desk, and I had to fight not to back up. "However, your dual heritage has saved you. This is Einar, Lord Nyström's son and heir. You're to wed him within the hour."

"What?" I looked between Harald and the other man. "What are you talking about?"

"As I've long suspected, you're not fit to bear the name berserker. But your nymph blood can serve a purpose. Due to a mistake in my youth, you are my sole heir and thus stand to inherit my lands and estate. I refuse to leave my legacy in your hands, so the only solution is to see you wed and bred. My grandsons will still carry your blood, but I trust it will be diluted enough not to matter."

My heart pounded so hard the room seemed to tilt. I couldn't have heard him correctly.

"You should be grateful Lord Nyström consented to this union. Einar is an accomplished warrior close to earning his thousandth kill."

I looked at Einar. "Congratulations. I'll jump from the Dragon Tower before I'll agree to marry you."

"Hold your tongue," Harald snapped. "Your opinion matters little in this arrangement and your wishes not at all. You're my responsibility, as well as my burden. My fellow lords have left it to me to decide your fate."

"I'm a drengr in the Holmgang," I fired back. "Only Hauk has the authority to say whether I can stay at Bjørneskalle."

A dangerous glint entered his eyes, and his tone turned silky. "You call him by his first name?"

My stomach clenched. With one word, I'd told him everything he needed to know about my relationship with the Hersir.

He spoke into my dismayed silence, his tone dripping with derision. "Your association with Sigridsson compromises his ability to be objective about your status. Perhaps you should have thought of that before you offered yourself to him. But I expect you couldn't help yourself, could you? It's in your blood."

Somehow, I managed to speak without screaming. "You're forgetting something. If you force me out of the Holmgang, I'll never gain my immortality."

He looked me straight in the eye. "I haven't forgotten. You'll age slowly. That should give you some comfort—and Einar ample time to take his pleasure."

The degrading words wormed into my brain, leaving me speechless. From the time I was a child, he'd made it clear he was disappointed in me. But until now, I hadn't understood how much he hated me.

He loathed me so much he wanted me dead. Worse, he wanted me to suffer. To be humiliated and belittled as nothing more than a sexual possession.

My own father. It was too much to take in.

He turned to Einar. "I'll leave you two to get acquainted, assuming you wish it?"

"Thank you, my lord," Einar rumbled. He ran a bold gaze down my body. "I do wish it."

"As I told your father, bedding her shouldn't be a hardship. Her mother was good for one thing and she did it well. I assume Elin shares that trait."

"I *hate* you," I hissed. If I'd had a knife, I would have plunged it into his heart.

He regarded me a moment. "Another shared trait." He nodded at Einar and left.

I stood motionless, my mind blank and my body numb. Maybe if I stood in the same spot long enough, the castle would eventually crumble around me.

Einar cleared his throat.

Slowly, I turned my head toward him.

He opened his mouth—

"Before you say anything," I said in a low voice, "you should know that I will never, ever marry you. And if Harald somehow succeeds in forcing me to an altar, you'd better never fall asleep. Because I will chop off your balls and watch you bleed out."

Now his mouth fell open.

"Go ahead. I didn't mean to interrupt."

He drew himself up. "I won't be insulted."

"Then you should probably leave." Because I had some creative ideas for other parts of his anatomy.

"You'll make a terrible wife."

"Count on it."

He looked like he might say more, but then he muttered something like "talk to my father" and swept from the room.

I let my shoulders sag as my bravado turned to defeat. He'd complain to Lord Nyström, who would send Harald and the other Rage Lords to truss me up and deliver me to Einar on a silver platter. With Hauk who knew where, I had nowhere to turn. No one to help me—

I gasped, the sound loud in the quiet room.

I had someone. I had Asher.

And he was just a Spruce door away.

CHAPTER
TEN

Ten minutes later, I stood in my room with my palms and forehead against the door. Tears burned my throat. I'd called for Asher every way I knew how. But the door was silent. It couldn't reach him.

I turned and gazed at the staff on the bed. The spear was gone, the wooden tip rounded off once more. "If you have any other tricks, now's not the time to be shy."

The staff didn't move.

My voice thickened. "I can't do this alone."

A knock at the door had me whirling around, my heart racing.

Hauk's urgent rumble drifted from the other side. "Elin?"

I flung open the door. He rushed inside, shut it, and gripped my arms. "Are you all right? I went to my office as soon as I could. I thought you'd gone with Einar."

Disgust made me shudder. "I'd rather die." Although, that was what Harald wanted. He just preferred I produce an heir first. My eyes stung.

"Hey," Hauk said softly. He pulled me against his chest, his big hand palming my head. "It's okay," he said gently. "It won't come to that."

"Can you talk to the other lords?" I lifted my head. "You're the Hersir. You could—"

"I tried." His eyes were bleak. "I explained that today wasn't your fault. But Harald made"—his gaze darkened—"accusations. He knows I can't lie outright. He made sure the Rage Lords know how I feel about you."

Humiliation coursed through me. Harald had forced him to tell the lords about the Dragon Tower...and what we did there. No wonder they were on board with me serving as Einar's broodmare. They thought I was a mindless, sex-crazed nymph. A perfect candidate for the job.

I pushed out of Hauk's arms and went to the bed, where I knelt and dragged my duffel from underneath.

"What are you doing?" he asked behind me.

"Leaving." I stood and dumped the duffel on the mattress. It wouldn't take long to pack. There was nothing from Bjørneskalle I wanted.

"Elin, stop."

"No time." Harald would be looking for me, if he wasn't already.

"You can't just walk out of the castle. The gate is under heavy guard. Provens patrol round the clock."

"I'll slip past them."

"You won't." Hauk grabbed my arm and spun me around. "Gods, Elin, who do you think is in charge of security around here? Bjørneskalle is protected by layers upon layers of enchantments. You won't get anywhere near the gate, let alone the wall."

"Well I have to try something!" I yanked out of his grip, my voice rising as frustration beat at me. "What do you want me to do? Marry Einar?"

"No. I want you to come on a quest with me."

I blinked at him. "A quest." He wanted me to assassinate a Mythical?

"The Rage Lords won't let you continue the Holmgang, but they can't stop you from going on a quest. Anyone can take a blood oath. It doesn't have to come from the Guild."

I thought it over. He was right, but... "I'm not trained, remember? I can't control my rage."

"You won't need rage magic. Not for this." He gripped my arms again, and a strong emotion burned in his eyes. "You won't even have to fight. You can fulfill your oath simply by showing up. I'll take care of the rest."

Unease crept over me. "What do you mean?"

"You know how my father's curse forces me to accept every quest I'm offered?"

I gave a tentative nod.

"There's one I've been putting off. For the first time, I worried I might not make it back alive. The Mythical I'm tasked with killing is Radegast."

"The Slavic god of hospitality?" He was a High Fae who shunned Faerie, opting to dwell on the human plane.

"That's the one." Hauk grimaced. "Except he's grown considerably inhospitable in recent decades. He's been amassing power and no one could figure out how since he doesn't have followers anymore. Then the Rage Lords learned he somehow came into possession of a Fae artifact called the Eternity Stone."

I'd never heard of it, but I could guess what it meant. "It makes him invincible?"

"Its most famous power is resurrection of the dead. But if you use it that way, it's a one-shot deal and the stone returns to Faerie. Radegast never resurrected anyone with it. He figured out that by keeping the stone for himself, he's truly immortal. As long as it's on his person, he can't be killed. You could chop off his head and he'll regenerate. The High Fae and the Rage Lords want the stone recovered. It belongs in Faerie, where it can be contained. Mythicals as a whole rarely agree on anything, but everyone sees Radegast as a threat. The stone gives him too much power, and it's driven him into madness. Lately, he's taken to killing humans and using their bodies to decorate his fortress."

I suppressed a shudder.

Hauk went on, and now excitement thrummed in his voice. "If I can get that stone, I'll have my immortality. I'll still have to accept any quest petitions that come my way, but at least I won't have to worry about dying while hunting some goblin through a Welsh bog."

"You could bypass your father's curse," I breathed. But how could I help him take on such a powerful immortal? I shook my head. "If I went with you, I'd be more of a liability than an asset."

"No," Hauk murmured, "you'd be my secret weapon. I've studied Radegast, learning as much as I can about his strengths and weaknesses. I can't kill him while he has the stone. My only hope is to distract him long enough to take it and render him vulnerable. In all my research, one thing kept popping up. Radegast has a deep fondness for nymphs. His orgies can last for days."

Ice slid through my veins. I'd been stupid. So very, very stupid.

Hauk frowned. "What's wrong?"

"You want me to sleep with him," I said, surprised at how normal my voice sounded.

"No!" He stooped a bit, his fingers tightening on my arms. "No, of course not. Just distract him long enough for me to grab the stone. You're a half-breed, so I wasn't sure if your nymph blood would be strong enough to keep his attention, but—"

"But you tried me out yourself and now you know I'm nymph enough after all." I pulled out of his hands as pieces clicked together in my head. "You planned this right from the start, pulling me off the practice field and taking me to your office. Offering me private training sessions in a place where no one would find us."

His frown deepened. "It wasn't like that—"

"You bought me pizza and I fell for it!" My heart pounded as the full weight of his deception sank in. "I bought your tragic childhood and asshole father life story hook, line, and sinker."

"Elin, will you listen," he growled. He reached for me, but I stumbled back.

"Don't *touch* me." I put up my hands. "You didn't take me to the Dragon Tower to train me. You took me there to see if I was fuckable enough to help you save your neck!"

His eyes flashed silver, his fists curling at his sides as though he fought to keep himself from grabbing me. "You're wrong about that," he said in a low growl. "I didn't need the tower to know you're fuckable. It's the only fucking thing I can think about when I'm near you."

My jaw dropped. "Is that supposed to make you sound better?"

"Do you want me to say you're repulsive? That I don't desire you? Because I can't say that, Elin, and neither can any other male with a pulse." His growl dropped a full octave. "You're a walking temptation. You've got these big, blue eyes a man could drown in and a body built for sin. You need only glance in my direction and I'm hard as a fucking anvil. And the way you move—" He cursed. "I'm attracted to you, but that's not why I want to see if there could be something more

between us. Now that I've talked to you—spent time with you
—I've seen your intelligence and your courage. You don't give
up, Elin, even when everyone around you tries to kick you back
down."

I stayed silent, letting the tension grow thicker.

"You felt our connection up on the tower," he said quietly.
"Don't try to deny it."

It didn't matter what I'd felt—or thought I'd felt. I could
lie, even if I was only lying to myself.

But he couldn't.

I held his stare. "Did you kiss me on the tower to see if I
was nymph enough to tempt Radegast?"

"What happened between us is bigger than this quest."

"Yes or no."

A muscle twitched in his cheek. "Don't do this, Elin."

"Just answer the question," I whispered.

"N—" He winced. "Fuck."

Somehow, I managed to keep standing even as a fist
squeezed my heart to pulp. He wasn't offering me a quest. He
was asking me to play prostitute to his pimp. It was no
different than Harald shoving me into Einar's bed.

But at least Harald was honest. He never pretended to feel
anything but contempt for me.

He never pretended to care.

A curious calm descended over me. I walked to the door
and rested my hand on the wood for a moment. When I turned
around, Hauk was just behind me, apprehension in his gaze.

"You should go," I told him. "My uncle will be here soon."

"What uncle?" He glanced at the door.

"My mother's brother is a satyr. He'll help me leave the
castle. The door said he's on his way."

His Adam's apple bobbed as he swallowed. "Elin—"

"I want you to go."

"You're making a mistake."

"No." I looked into his eyes, my gaze as steady as my resolve. "I did that earlier today, when I met you on that tower." I opened the door and stepped aside.

He stared at me with a clenched jaw.

Then he left, his booted footsteps as sharp as the knife in my heart.

CHAPTER
ELEVEN

I shut the door and leaned against it. My heart raced, but my eyes were dry. Hauk Sigridsson didn't deserve my tears—and I didn't have time to indulge in them.

I took several deep breaths to slow my galloping pulse, then faced the wood and pressed my palms flat against the surface. "Let's try this one more time," I murmured, closing my eyes. "Please, Brother Spruce, find Asher Greenleaf. Tell him his niece needs him urgently."

The wood warmed against my skin. In my head, a series of images flashed. *A forest full of trees. Rolling hills covered in wildflowers. A green meadow winding past a river—*

I dropped my hands, severing the connection. My throat burned, the tears I'd held at bay threatening to come. The door showed me the places it searched for Asher.

And all of them were empty.

I was truly on my own.

But I couldn't dwell on that, either. My hour was almost up.

I went to the bed and rummaged through my duffel bag. I

couldn't take it with me—I needed to travel as light as possible if I hoped to leave the castle without getting caught. But there was one item I couldn't leave behind.

My fingers brushed something hard and round.

I withdrew my mother's mirror and stared at the vines engraved in the silver.

My heart pounded.

No time for this.

Harald would be looking for me.

I flipped the mirror open.

She sat on the tree stump, her curves wrapped in a brilliant green dress. She faced away, her head tilted to one side, her reddish-brown curls piled high on her crown. The gown's corset boning was visible through the fabric, and the full skirt fanned around her.

She did that sometimes—wore clothes from previous centuries. But she was always stunning.

"Mom?"

She rose and spun around, her skirts stirring the leaves. "Elin!" She clasped her hands together. "Oh, I've missed you, sweetheart."

I gripped the mirror so hard my fingers turned white.

"You must tell me what you've been up to," she said. "I want to hear everything."

"The Hersir pretended to be interested in me so I'd help him defeat a High Fae who has the power of immortality. I…" My voice caught. "I liked him."

"That's wonderful! Tell me more."

I closed my eyes. I couldn't tell her about Harald's plan for me. Couldn't say those awful words aloud. "That's it," I whispered.

"I'm glad you told me."

I opened my eyes as she flashed a dazzling smile. "I want to share something with you. May I?" When I gave no reply, she lowered her voice like she was sharing a juicy secret. "I'm going to sing you a song."

I squeezed the mirror. Over the years, I'd poured my heart out when we spoke. I'd choked back tears when Harald sent me to bed without dinner. In hushed, nervous tones, I'd confessed to sleeping with Nils. I'd sobbed uncontrollably, my words incoherent, the night Fiona died.

But my mother's response was always the same. She was as steady and certain as the sun. And as indifferent.

She began singing, her voice pure and sweet.

Ash and oak and willow, three
Which one shall my dearest be?
Oh, ash with leaves the first to fall
And ancient oak, its branches tall . . .

The song was beautiful.

And empty.

I brought the mirror to my face. "Will you shut up?" I hissed. "Why can't you ever just listen!"

She finished. "Well? Did you like it?"

A harsh laugh ripped from my throat. "*No.* I fucking hate it!" My voice rose. "Why can't you be real? Why can't you be here?"

Her delicate eyebrows pulled together, and she blushed. "It sounds better in Gaelic..."

I barely heard her. My heart was racing. *Why can't she be here?*

She could. She could be here.

I could bring her back.

All I had to do was help Hauk defeat Radegast. He'd said the Eternity Stone could make its owner immortal—or bring someone back from the dead.

"Look at me," my mother laughed, brushing leaves from her gown. "Such a mess."

Excitement hummed in my veins. I could do it. I could pull her from the mirror and make her real.

"I wouldn't be alone," I said.

She looked up, smiling. "Of course."

"I have to go." My heart skipped a beat. "I'll see you soon." I closed the mirror, stuffed it in my pocket, and headed for the door.

Halfway there, I swung around, rushed back to the bed, and snatched the staff from the mattress. I raced to the door and yanked it open.

Nils nearly crashed through the opening.

I jumped back. "What the— *Nils?*"

"Elin!" He caught himself against the jamb, his big body filling the doorway.

"What are you doing here?"

"I came with Harald."

I gasped and looked over his shoulder, expecting to see the Rage Lords looming behind him.

"It's all right," he said quickly. "I'm alone." His gaze darted to the staff in my hand, and he lowered his voice. "I know what you're planning, and you can't go through with it. You can't trust Sigridsson, Elin. This quest is too dangerous."

My guard went up. "How do you know about that?"

"I eavesdropped." At my indrawn breath, he rushed on. "I was just trying to protect you! I was watching your room, ready to intercept Harald if he came to your door. I was going to claim I saw you leave and hopefully buy you some time."

Gratitude swept me. He'd put himself—and his job—at considerable risk. I knew how much he valued his position with Harald, and how badly he wanted to escape the shadow of his father's scandal. "Thank you," I said. "You have no idea how much your help means to me."

"Then let me keep helping." His gaze searched my face. "You don't have to do this thing for Sigridsson."

"I'm not doing it for him."

"You think he's your only option, but he's not. I could—"

"I have my own reasons for going," I said, impatience beating at me. "I appreciate you looking out for me, but I have to go." I tried to duck around him, but he blocked the door.

"Elin, wait."

"I have to go." I tried again.

He moved with me, his body like a boulder. "Just hear me out."

I couldn't get past him. I was trapped and out of time. I raised the staff.

"I love you," he blurted.

I froze, my eyes wide. I couldn't have heard him right. Nils didn't love me. Our teenage fumblings were years in the past, and he'd had plenty of girlfriends since then. It was his ambition that kept him working for Harald. There was no other reason for him to stay at Berregaard Manor...

My thoughts trailed off as he stared down at me, his brown eyes raw and intense.

Oh no. How could I have been so blind? But the answer was simple. I'd spent my time at the manor training. As the years passed and I failed to master my rage, the threat of death had loomed larger.

Romance had been the last thing on my mind. I'd been focused on keeping my head.

A flush spread over his cheeks. "I've loved you since we were kids. You were my first, you know. But it was more than just sex for me."

"Nils—"

"You could be happy with me, Elin. I'll take care of you."

My stomach clenched. He was handsome and kind, and he deserved someone who loved him with a soul-searing passion. The love I'd felt for him at sixteen had been like a meteor—a fiery streak that burned bright for a brief moment and then faded from sight.

I took a deep breath. "I'm flattered, Nils, and...touched. But you're my—"

"Don't." He closed his eyes on a long blink. When he opened them, pain gathered in his gaze. "Don't give me the friend talk."

Silence fell. "I'm sorry," I said quietly. "I didn't know you felt this way."

His gaze hardened. "He's using you. No matter what he says, Sigridsson is only in this for himself."

"I know that." Irritation spilled into my voice. "I'm using him, too. Now I need you to let me pass. If you care about me at all, Nils, you have to let me get to Hauk. He's my only way out of Bjørneskalle."

He frowned, and I could almost see the indecision churning in his mind.

"Do you want to see me married to Einar?" I asked. "To watch me live out my days as a combination sex slave and baby machine?"

"Of course not," he rasped.

"Then let me go."

He stepped aside.

Relief had me zipping past him. On impulse, I swiveled back and gave him a peck on the cheek. "Thank you, Nils," I said breathlessly, then hefted the staff and rushed down the hall.

"Hurry," he urged after me.

I slowed just enough to turn and wave, glimpsing him standing with his hand over the spot I'd kissed.

Regret sliced through me, but I pushed it aside as I ran down the steps and entered the main part of the castle. I went as fast as I dared, ducking into the shadows any time I heard footsteps or the sound of voices. My heart pounded and my palms grew damp, making it hard to grip the staff.

I darted past the Great Hall and flew down another set of stairs. More hallways. More twists and turns.

Almost there. The Norsemen loomed ahead, their tall forms on either side of the arch leading to the Hersir's Tower.

Freedom beckoned.

A shout went up behind me.

I whirled, my heart hammering. At the other end of the corridor stood Harald and half a dozen tall, menacing males. Their powerful bodies were wrapped in leather, their hair cascading down their backs in a riot of battle braids. Each one held a broadsword in a massive fist.

The Rage Lords had found me, and they looked ready to kill.

Harald flicked his sword, sending blue fire sizzling down the blade. "Enough games, Elin," he said, his voice echoing off the stone. "You try my patience."

I looked between him and the Norsemen, and my heart sank. Even if I managed to sprint to the statues before he reached me, I'd have to stop and get permission to pass.

"You won't make it," he said, guessing the direction of my thoughts. "Spare yourself the humiliation of being run to ground."

Why, so he could humiliate me by dragging me to a farce of a wedding ceremony?

He advanced slowly, his sword wreathed in rage. "There's nothing in that tower for you anyway. Sigridsson left."

My chest tightened. Hauk was gone?

Harald kept coming. "Did you think he would save you? Swoop in like a knight in a fairy tale? That ridiculous Brownie filled your head with nonsense. The High Fae take what they want and move on." His pale eyes glinted. "And it appears Sigridsson got what he wanted from you."

I bit back a gasp. Even after a lifetime of enduring his scorn, his cruelty took my breath away.

He stopped, his blade hissing and crackling with power. We faced each other with nothing but the stretch of flagstones between us.

"You're my father," I said, hating how my voice broke at the end. "Couldn't you have loved me just a little?"

Our gazes held. Then his lips curved in a rare smile, and the look he gave me was almost indulgent. "Ah, Elin, if only there was something about you to love."

The words hit me like a slap, the blow so forceful I took a step back.

He started toward me again. Behind him, the other lords moved, too.

On instinct, I flung up my hand holding the staff. The wood stayed dormant and cold.

Harald's sword blazed brighter.

I whirled and ran.

Everything seemed to happen in slow motion. As I neared the Norsemen, movement on the stairs behind them caught my eye.

Hauk descended the spiral staircase, his tattered brown cloak floating behind him. He hit the ground with a bellow, one hand stretched toward me.

I lengthened my strides.

Footsteps pounded at my back.

Hauk burst between the Norsemen. In one movement, he

grabbed me, flung out his free hand, and gritted his teeth. The air turned wavy, rippling out like a stone tossed on the surface of a lake.

Harald and the lords charged toward us. "Stop!" Harald shouted, his features contorted in fury. "Don't you dare use that portal!"

Hauk gripped my arm and tossed me through.

CHAPTER

TWELVE

W ind howled around me, ripping at my hair and
clothes. *Can't see.* I stood in an abyss, a hurricane
screaming in my ears. A thousand tiny needles stung
my skin. Just when I opened my mouth to scream, it stopped.

The loss of pressure was so abrupt, I staggered and fell, my
palms landing in...grass?

I lifted my head and gasped.

A green meadow spread before me, its gentle hills rolling
toward a purple horizon. Wherever I was, it was twilight. The
purple spread across the sky and cast a soft glow over the
ground.

I looked around for the staff, but it was nowhere to be
found. My heart sank. I'd lost it in the portal, which meant I
was unlikely to see it again. It could be on a hundred different
planes.

The air rippled, and then Hauk stepped onto the grass like
someone leaving an elevator. Unlike me, he didn't trip or
stumble.

"Elin!" He rushed over and helped me up. "Are you all right?"

"I think so." I stepped back, putting distance between us. "I've never felt a portal like that before." Normally, traveling between planes was like walking from one room to the next.

His expression darkened. "My father's doing. To be honest, I wasn't sure he'd allow us in. He made his point by leaving me in the void a bit longer than you."

I turned in a slow circle. "We're in Faerie?"

He gave a murmur of assent. "Underhill. Realm of the Sidhe or Aos Sí. The lands of the Tuatha Dé Danann, although my father has never counted himself one of them."

I faced him. "Who is he?"

"Crom Cruach."

My heart skipped a beat, and it took me a couple tries to form a response. "Your father is the Irish god of human sacrifice?"

"I told you he thrives on cruelty."

That was an understatement. Crom Cruach was a Faerie supervillain. Whereas most High Fae downplayed their bad past conduct, he seemed to relish his evil reputation. Rumors had swirled about him for centuries, even up to modern times. There was the occasional kidnapping—something Hauk's mother's story seemed to confirm—but there were also whispers he still actively recruited followers. The High Fae had agreed to discourage worship years ago. Crom Cruach apparently hadn't received the memo.

And he was too powerful for any High Fae to stand up to him. The ancient ones could have probably taken him on if they banded together, but they didn't typically cooperate that way. They preferred to let berserkers do their dirty work for them.

"What are you thinking?" Hauk asked, pulling me from my musings.

I hesitated.

"I'm not like my father," he said quietly. "It's one of the reasons he hates me so much."

I could certainly identify with that, and I wasn't about to accuse him of the atrocities Crom was known for.

But Hauk had lied to me—or at least skirted the truth. He'd befriended me, leading me to believe our shared status as half-breeds gave us a special bond.

And he'd seduced me to test my sex appeal. If that raven hadn't interrupted us, I would have slept with him. I would have trusted him with my body even as he prepared to use it as a means to an end.

He stepped toward me. "Elin—"

"Why did you come back to Bjørneskalle?" I demanded. "Harald said you were gone."

"He lied. I never left." Hauk's voice went raspy. "I was coming to fetch you. I decided I couldn't leave you behind."

"Because you want me to seduce Radegast."

"Because I *care* about you," he insisted, a growl in his voice. "I made a mistake and I admitted it. When are you going to stop punishing me for it?"

I folded my arms. "Me not trusting you isn't a punishment, Hauk. It's self-preservation. Maybe you didn't lie directly, but you didn't tell the truth, either. You should have told me about Radegast from the beginning."

As I spoke, my conscience twinged. I was angry at him for deceiving me, but I was deceiving him, too. At this very moment. I wanted to take down Radegast so I could get the Eternity Stone and bring back my mother.

Which would leave Hauk stuck with his father's curse.

"You're right," he said, regret in his eyes. "I should have

told you. All I can do now is promise I won't betray your trust again." He swept his cloak back, revealing a broadsword strapped to his side. He also wore the obsidian dagger around his thigh, the naked blade gleaming black in the meadow's soft light.

He drew the sword, planted it point first in the grass, and knelt. "I vow it, Elin Berregaard. I'll protect you with my life. And from this day forward I'll always be completely honest with you."

My breath caught. A vow like that was no small thing, especially in Faerie. Words had power. If he betrayed me, he'd be forsworn. The consequences could be deadly.

He stood and sheathed his sword. "I don't expect you to help me with Radegast."

"No," I said, "I need this quest. I'm done letting Harald dictate my future."

Approval gleamed in his blue eyes. "All right, then. You've got yourself a quest."

"But..." I cleared my throat as heat rushed into my cheeks. "I have conditions."

"Go on."

"I won't sleep with him." I lifted my chin. "Or you."

The approval shifted, and something hot and knowing appeared. "Understood."

My blood heated as desire bloomed low in my belly. I curled my hand into a fist, letting my nails dig into my palm. I had to resist him and the effect he had on me. Regardless of his vow, I couldn't let myself be swayed by him again.

There was too much at stake.

A woman's high-pitched laugh rang out.

I jumped.

Hauk drew his sword.

On a hill in the distance sat a house—a Georgian mansion

that had most definitely not been there a moment ago. As if someone flipped a switch, the purple twilight lifted and a bright midday sun filled the sky.

Hauk looked at me with grim eyes. "My father is home, and it appears he's agreed to speak with us."

CHAPTER
THIRTEEN

I stared at the mansion. "So why are we in Faerie, again?"

Hauk sheathed his sword. "I need to know where to find Radegast. He's aware the High Fae put a bounty on his head, so he's been hiding."

"And you think Crom knows where he is?"

He nodded. "Whether he'll tell me is a different story."

The woman's laughter rang out again, sending a chill down my spine. It was too loud, the garish sound at odds with the pastoral scenery.

"Have you been to Faerie before?" Hauk asked.

"Just a few times as a child. My uncle had some centaur friends who lived in a big forest. He used to take them weed."

Hauk raised his eyebrows. "He sounds interesting."

"You have no idea."

"I probably don't have to tell you this, but don't eat anything while you're here. And no accepting gifts. Being half-breeds, you and I should be immune from High Fae tricks, but my father's realm is unpredictable." He looked at the mansion. "To say the least," he muttered.

I followed his gaze, wishing I had the staff. It was unpredictable, too.

"Come on," he murmured. "And stay close."

We walked side by side, our boots soundless in the lush grass. The mansion loomed, three stories of red brick surrounded by precise box hedges cut into geometrical patterns. Gleaming windows reflected the sun. It was beautiful, but...

An unsettled feeling drifted down my spine.

And then I realized why.

It was *too* beautiful. Too perfect. In the real world, bricks were weathered. Shingles got stained by rain or faded by the sun. Windows had streaks. But this mansion was pristine—a Barbie house on a spread of grass that looked like it had been trimmed with scissors.

The laughter echoed around us, and a woman peeked her head over a tall hedge. I got a glimpse of yellow hair and a dark blue feather before she dropped out of sight.

I tensed.

Hauk spoke under his breath. "It's all right. Remember, you're Fae, too."

Not like this. Not like him. My family members talked to trees and danced naked in the moonlight.

More laughter. I clenched my jaw. The sound was jarring, like someone imitating what they *thought* a laugh should sound like.

We reached a walkway—or maybe one appeared out of thin air. Just as suddenly, there was fine gravel under our boots. It led to a white front door adorned with a shiny brass knocker in the form of a cherub.

A woman strolled out from one of the hedges. Her hair was the color of a tennis ball and arranged in a mass that defied gravity. A large blue feather stuck out from one side. The rich color matched her dress, which looked like something Marie Antoinette would have worn. Ruffles spilled down the front of a stiff skirt shaped like a bell. More ruffles decorated the edge of the parasol she carried over one shoulder.

"Ah, a nymph!" she exclaimed, strolling toward us. Her beautiful face blossomed into a warm, inviting smile. "What a treat."

Hauk stopped, bringing me to a halt beside him.

The woman reached us and made a low curtsy. "Lord Hauk, it's been an age." Her corset gaped away from her chest, revealing impressive cleavage and rouged nipples. When she straightened, her face changed. The shift was abrupt, like an out of order frame in a movie reel. Her expression was serene— and then it wasn't. For the briefest second, something vicious and feral flashed in her face, and I got the impression of glowing eyes and far too many teeth.

As quickly as it came, it was gone, and she was lovely once more.

My heart rate sped up.

"Morgana," Hauk said, offering her a formal bow. "Is he accepting visitors?"

She tipped her head to the side, making the feather curl against her cheek. A beauty patch near her mouth lifted as she smiled. "If it was just you, I'd have to say no." Her gaze shifted to me. "But since you've brought one so lovely, I think he'll make an exception."

He gave her another bow, then took my elbow and guided me up the walkway. As we approached the front steps, the mansion's white door swung open of its own accord.

I glanced over my shoulder.

Morgana was gone.

"Pay her no mind," Hauk murmured. "Focus on what's in front of you. Don't get distracted."

A shiver lifted the hairs on my nape, and I moved closer to him as we climbed the steps and entered a black and white checkered foyer. It was as immaculate as the mansion's exterior.

And just as unsettling.

The floor stretched in all directions, extending so far in front of us the sides narrowed to a point in the distance.

I gazed around, my heart thumping painfully in my chest. "What do we do now?" I whispered.

Hauk's hand found mine at my side. "We keep moving."

I curled my fingers around his. My resolve to keep him at arm's length could wait. Right now, his presence was like a life preserver in a sea of uncertainty.

As we had in the grass outside, we continued walking forward. This time, however, the scenery didn't change. We seemed to walk for hours. My heels burned inside my boots and a trickle of sweat snaked down my back. I hadn't eaten since lunch on the Dragon Tower earlier in the day.

Or was that yesterday? So much had happened, I couldn't keep track anymore. And time passed differently in Faerie. A few seconds could be centuries in human time. It could also be days...or a month.

Just when I was ready to tell Hauk we should give up, noise to my left made me freeze.

Enormous gilt doors stood ajar. Through them, a man sat at a desk, his head bent over a document as he wrote with a quill. The scratching sound echoed across the foyer.

Hauk squeezed my hand. "Whatever happens, don't leave my side."

Nerves jangling, I nodded.

He led me to the doors, pushed one open, and escorted me inside.

The room was clearly a study—the kind used by noblemen

in past centuries. The furniture was ornate, with delicate legs and carved decorations. Behind the desk, French doors led to a wide terrace splashed with sunlight.

The man spoke without looking up. "I know why you're here, and I'm afraid I can't help you." His accent was Irish yet not Irish. Like Asher's, it held something far older. The cadence was almost musical.

Hauk moved us forward until we stood a few steps from the desk. "Can't or won't?" he asked.

The man threw down his quill and stood.

I caught my breath—and realized I was truly seeing him for the first time. Through glamour or some trick, he'd made himself the least interesting thing in the room.

But not now.

Now, it was impossible to look away. Well over six feet tall, he was Disney prince perfect, with deep blue eyes and sculpted lips. His long blond hair was swept back from a broad forehead, and his chiseled jaw held just enough golden stubble to stop him from being too pretty.

And that was just his face.

Black pants hugged powerful thighs that led to knee-high riding boots. His white shirt was unbuttoned, exposing a smooth, tan chest. The hollow of his throat was curiously sensual—a gentle dip that moved as he spoke.

Wait, he's speaking?

I forced my gaze from his throat. As I did, it was like someone snapped their fingers, restoring the sound in the room.

"—and you made your choice a long time ago."

Beside me, Hauk stiffened. "It's hardly fair to deny me help when you're the one who cursed me in the first place."

The man smirked. "*Fair.* You sound like a human." He

looked at me. "Now, here's one who understands all too well that life isn't fair."

Time stopped. Or maybe it just no longer mattered. Nothing did, really, because the most amazing man was looking at me like I was the only woman in the world.

"You could be, you know," he said.

And just like that, we were on the terrace.

Alone.

Panic flooded me. I spun around. Hauk was gone, the room empty.

"Don't worry about him."

I turned, my heart fluttering like a wild creature in my chest.

Crom Cruach—because it couldn't be anyone else—stood on the edge of the terrace. Except it wasn't a terrace any longer. Now it was a balcony. The genteel decorations were gone, replaced with rough stone.

He was different, too. His hair was longer and tied back from his face with a strip of leather. Instead of the open shirt and riding boots, he wore red armor the color of blood. I looked closer.

Okay, that was real blood.

His blue eyes found mine, and my heart skipped a beat. His resemblance to Hauk was uncanny.

"Actually," he said, "Hauk resembles *me*."

I swallowed a gasp. "You can read my mind."

He inclined his head. "You'll need to work on shielding your thoughts if you want to kill Radegast."

"I thought you said you can't help us."

Crom sighed, and the movement made his armor glisten. Bile burned my throat.

"Come," he said, extending a gauntleted hand. "I want to show you something."

I didn't move. "Where's Hauk?"

He frowned. For the briefest moment, I got a glimpse of why it would be *very* stupid to cross him. His expression darkened, and his blue eyes turned empty and black.

Then his anger cleared, and he waved me forward. "Come, come, I'm not going to harm you."

My feet wanted to stay put, but I forced myself to approach him. His gauntlet *melted* away as I put my hand in his.

He pulled me to the balcony's railing and braced his hands on the stone.

I looked over the edge, and my stomach dropped. We had to be hundreds of feet in the air. Far below, a battle raged. Everywhere I looked, men in armor clashed. Humans and Mythicals scattered the field.

That meant the scene had to be a memory. It had been thousands of years since men and Mythicals lived openly alongside each other. They fought as one now, centaurs and Fae, humans in conical helmets and leather armor. Giants strode through the mix, swinging axes the size of boulders. Berserkers sliced their way through the melee, blue fire licking over their swords. Wizards in long robes cupped balls of light in their hands, then hurled them at the enemy.

Horses galloped around the edges, their riders carrying pennants that snapped in the wind. The ground underfoot ran red. Men screamed. Metal clanged. The thick, coppery scent of blood reached my nose.

"Exquisite, isn't it?" Crom looked over the field, his expression almost lustful. He closed his eyes and inhaled. "All that *life* in the air."

"It looks like death to me."

He opened his eyes and gave me a patient look. "Ah, Elin, don't you see? It's one and the same."

I held my tongue. It seemed like a bad idea to argue with a guy wearing blood armor.

"You don't like the battle?" His tone was polite, as if we were discussing our favorite foods or the types of television shows we liked to watch.

Not that he even knew what TV was.

He tsked. "You make assumptions. That's dangerous."

I bit my lip. He'd read my mind again. "I'm sorry."

He waved it off. "I'm actually quite interested in television. Video games specifically." He smiled, looking more like Hauk than ever. "I've experienced something of a renaissance thanks to gamers. Humans do love a villain." He turned and leaned against the railing. "Did you know some of these young people will spend all day gaming? I mean hours and hours. They worship the stuff. I get more juice from them than a whole village of druids." His tone turned musing. "It really makes you wonder about the state of parenting today."

I almost choked. He'd stripped his own son of immortality, and he had *thoughts* on modern parenting?

"I see Hauk's been filling your head with tales," he said.

"You cursed him because he wouldn't stay in Faerie. Don't you think that's a little harsh?"

Crom shrugged. "He's an ungrateful child—a character flaw all my children share, unfortunately."

Hauk had siblings? Although, it made sense. Crom was thousands of years old. And he had a habit of kidnapping wives.

"Now I *know* you've been fed a line of bullshit. Sigrid came here of her own free will." He shuddered—and the reaction seemed genuine. "Anyone's who ever met that female knows she's as stubborn as a pixie. It's not my fault she wouldn't be reasonable during the divorce negotiations."

"So you kept her prisoner?"

"I like to think of it as an opportunity for extended reflection."

A warm breeze drifted across the balcony, bringing a fresh wave of blood-soaked air. Crom turned and gazed at the field. As he did, he seemed to become *more*. More solid. More vivid and powerful.

This was probably as close to his true form as I'd ever see.

He looked at me, a little smile playing around his mouth. "Not quite, Elin," he murmured. Then he dropped his glamour.

His blond hair gleamed like spun gold. A crown of flowers and vines perched on his head, and his skin glowed like it was lit from within. Pointed ears peeked from his curls, which fell loose around his shoulders and cascaded to his waist.

But the hair didn't make him feminine. On the contrary, he was fierce. Beautiful and deadly. His features were sharper, like clay that had been chiseled with a knife. Impossibly blue eyes —haughty and cruel—stared back at me.

Predator.

Alien.

I knew instinctively that if he parted those full, sensual lips, pointed teeth would greet me. The being behind those eyes didn't have the same kinds of emotions as other people— even other Mythicals. It *chose* to play along in society. And it could choose to stop playing whenever it wished.

In a blink, his glamour was back in place.

I released a shaky breath.

He brushed the back of his hand across my cheek.

When did he get so close?

"Why so frightened?" he murmured. "We're not all that different, you and I." He tipped my chin up and made a throaty sound of appreciation. "Daughter of rage and beauty. You might be surprised what you see if you ever bother to really look in that mirror."

"I..." Warmth curled in my belly. When I spoke next, it seemed as if my voice came from far away. "I don't know what you mean."

"Of course not," he whispered. "Stay with me and I'll show you." He turned my head so I faced the study, which was now a ballroom filled with people. Couples in Georgian costume whirled in a waltz, the ladies' gowns billowing like colorful flowers. The gentlemen wore powered wigs tied back with satin ribbons. In the corner, a group of musicians bent over violins, the music mingling with the dancers' laughter.

Crom turned me again, and now I gazed upon the terrace. The balcony and battle were long gone, replaced with a bright green lawn and a huge outdoor fountain. Nude women frolicked in the lower basin, giggling and splashing each other. One scooped water into her hands and let it cascade down her neck and breasts, her head tipped back on a contented sigh.

Naiads. Asher called them "water humpers."

Asher. My uncle... A memory tugged at me. Wasn't there something I was supposed to be doing?

Warm fingers caressed my cheek. Crom drew my attention back to him.

Beautiful. He was so beautiful. Was this what I was supposed to be doing?

"It could be," he said, smiling. "Stay with me. I'll make you a queen. It's all here, Elin. Yours for the taking. No more fighting, no need to chase after immortality."

Immortality...

That word was important. There *was* something I was supposed to do—some task I needed to complete.

I struggled against the lassitude that threatened to swamp me.

A task... There was a task.

No. Not a task. A *quest*.

Hauk.

My head cleared.

Crom narrowed his eyes.

"Hauk." I pulled my chin from Crom's grasp. "I'm here for Hauk."

The music stopped. The dancers froze. Outside, the naiads gasped and paused their play.

Crom's expression darkened. He lifted a hand.

I flinched, braced for a blow, but he merely ran a fingertip down my jaw.

A vivid image sprang into my mind. The two of us were nude in a huge bed with black silk sheets, our bodies slicked with sweat as we fucked ferociously—him on his back and me astride him. My spine was arched, my hips rolling in wild abandon. He gripped me around the waist, slamming me onto his thrusting cock over and over again. I bounced hard, my breasts jiggling and my mouth open on an unrestrained wail.

"It could be that way all the time," he murmured in my ear, and suddenly the image was gone and I was staring at the mansion's ceiling with my back pressed against his chest and intense pleasure throbbing between my legs. His voice slid into my head. "I could make you come, fair Elin."

My sex clamped so hard I cried out. Moisture soaked my panties. My head lolled on his shoulder, and I panted like an animal in heat. "What are you..." A wave of raw lust pummeled me, and I moaned loudly, my hips rolling. "What are you doing?"

"Merely showing you possibilities." He remained behind me, his chest rumbling against my back. "We could be spectacular together." His lips brushed my neck, and his voice became an echoing whisper. "Look."

More images flashed in my head, each one more erotic than the last. Me nude and spread on his lap as he sat on a golden throne, his lips at my neck and his hand petting my clit. Me naked and bent over a crowded banquet table as he drove into me from behind. Me facedown on a bed, my ass thrust high as he pounded my rear passage. Me on all fours with a collar around my neck, breasts swaying as I ate from his outstretched hand.

"That one's my favorite," he growled in my ear, and I was staring at the ceiling once more, my body on fire.

And he wasn't even touching me.

"I will," he said. "I'll touch you everywhere, my beauty." A phantom tongue dragged over my clit. It slid between my ass cheeks and swirled over my most secret, forbidden place before swooping back down. "Inside and outside, I'll make you mine."

I moaned, my sex clenching repeatedly. Goosebumps rushed over my skin. I squeezed my eyes shut as my body threatened to fly apart.

"Stay with me, Elin," he murmured, and the ghostly tongue worked my clit faster. "You'll want for nothing."

Except my freedom.

My eyes flew open.

With a strangled cry, I wrenched away from him. I stumbled and whirled, my chest heaving. "No!"

In my peripheral vision, the naiads scrambled from the fountain and scurried away, their bare feet soundless on the grass.

I clenched my fists at my sides as I squared off with Crom, who was dressed as a nobleman once more. His blue eyes—so like Hauk's—glittered with lust. "I like you angry," he said. "If you were mine, I'd endeavor to keep you that way often. All that delicious passion just under the surface. I'd wring it from you, goddess. They'd hear your screams throughout Faerie."

A fresh image appeared in my mind, this one sharper and more detailed than the others. I lay nude on the black silk with thick restraints at my wrists and ankles. My arms stretched over my head, and my nipples were caught in silver clamps connected by a jeweled chain. My legs were splayed so wide the tendons in my thighs strained. Red streaks crisscrossed my skin. Crom knelt between my thighs with a riding crop in one hand. He used his other to work a thick rubber cock into my glistening sex. His arm flew, bringing the crop down on my swollen clit. I drew a breath to scream—

—and faced him across the terrace, my sex smarting and my nipples tingling from the imaginary clamps. I gritted my teeth. "Stay out of my head!" As the last word echoed, we were on the ancient balcony again. I clutched at the stone, disoriented and flushed with desire.

Crom stood a short distance away, his face in profile as he gazed at the horizon. A gentle wind buffeted his hair, which was loose around his shoulders. The tip of a pointed ear showed through the golden mass. He was achingly beautiful.

And so very dangerous.

"So is Radegast," he said, turning his head toward me. His tone was conversational, as if he hadn't just pummeled my brain with sexual fantasies. "It's a fool's errand to take him on. If you enter his realm with your mind as unguarded as it's been with me, he'll read you like a book and have you for dinner. And he likes to play with his food."

My lust turned to ash as fear gripped me. Crom had manipulated my body as easily as a child playing with a doll. If Radegast was even a fraction as powerful, I was in serious trouble. But I couldn't return to Bjørneskalle. Even if I could, I needed the Eternity Stone. It was the only way to bring my mother ba—

I shoved the thought aside.

But it was too late. Crom clucked his tongue. "Ahh, quite

the plot you've devised, fair Elin. Whatever will Hauk think when he finds out you deceived him?"

I licked my lips, which had gone dry. "He'll understand." He was already living. My mother's life had been brutally cut short.

Crom tilted his head. "How did she die?"

"A car crash. I was six months old."

"An immortal nymph struck down in a motor car accident?"

"It plunged off the side of a mountain." According to Asher, who'd raced to the scene before the human authorities could discover her body, fire had consumed everything. Not even a Mythical could survive that.

Crom studied me a moment. "Do you care for my son?" he asked.

"He's a friend."

"Nothing more?"

I hesitated. Was this another game? His demeanor was different now, his tone one of a concerned father. It would probably be a mistake to believe it was genuine.

A smile teased his lips. "Probably," he murmured, and he was in front of me again, his hand grasping my jaw. "But you didn't answer my question."

"I..." *Did* I care for Hauk? My mind whirled as I tried to figure out how I felt without revealing my thoughts. I was attracted to him. I couldn't deny that. But he'd also led me on so he could assess my ability to seduce Radegast. Yes, he claimed he'd felt a connection once he got to know me, but that could be a lie, too.

"It's complicated," Crom said, clearly reading my mind. He sighed. "Love always is."

"I don't love him."

He spoke as if he hadn't heard me. "I'm giving you this

against my better judgment. Remember that."

Giving me what? Panic streaked down my spine. It was never good to accept gifts from the High Fae. They could use it as an excuse to claim you owed them something.

"You can pass it on to Hauk if you wish." The side of his mouth quirked up. "I'm sure he'll appreciate it."

"What do you—"

He pulled my face to his and kissed me.

I gasped, unwittingly giving him more access.

He took it, plunging his tongue deep.

My hands flew to his wrist, protests crowding my throat. Before I could push away, *knowledge* landed on my tongue. One second, I had no idea where Radegast lived. The next, I knew the exact coordinates for his castle. I couldn't have written them down. I couldn't picture them in my mind.

But I *knew* them. Because Crom Cruach had just placed them on my tongue.

He continued plundering my mouth. As he did, his voice echoed in my mind.

"If you ever grow tired of assassinations, my offer stands. And take this with you. It clashes with my decor."

I pushed at his chest—

—and stumbled into the twilight-drenched meadow with the staff in my hand.

Hauk sprang up from where he'd been sitting in the grass.

I doubled over, one hand braced on my knee as I tried to catch my breath.

Hauk gripped my shoulders and pulled me up. "Did he hurt you?" he demanded, steel in his voice.

"No," I panted, some instinct making me keep Crom's sexual slideshow to myself. "He told me where Radegast is."

Hauk's gaze touched on the staff. Then he looked at the mansion in the distance. "Let's go," he muttered. He put out a hand and began to open a portal. "We both need food and rest, and I'll feel better away from this place."

"Where are we going?"

He looked down at me as the air began to ripple. "How do you feel about Paris?"

CHAPTER

FOURTEEN

W e emerged in a modern-looking hallway lined with numbered doors. The carpet was plush, and the walls were covered in silk paper with an understated but stylish design.

"Is this a hotel?" I asked.

"Apartment building," Hauk said, producing a key. "This one's mine."

Surprise flitted through me. "You have an apartment?"

"Several." He unlocked the door and held it open. "I like having somewhere besides Bjørneskalle to crash in between quests."

As I stepped inside, lights sprang to life, illuminating a small but stylish living room with an attached kitchen. Long curtains swept across the far wall.

He closed the door and flipped the deadbolt. Then he strode to the curtains and pulled them back, revealing a huge window and a pair of sliding glass doors. "But I got this place for the view."

I caught my breath. The Eiffel Tower filled the night sky, its elegant lines lit by golden spotlights. "You have the Eiffel Tower outside your apartment," I breathed.

He shrugged out of his cloak. "There's a balcony, but it's probably too cold to sit outside." He frowned. "Assuming we didn't lose any time in Faerie." He went to a TV stand decked out with several video game consoles and digital displays. "It's still the same day," he said, relief in his voice.

My stomach growled.

Amusement gleamed in his eyes. "You sit. I'll find us something to eat." He tossed the cloak on a chair and went to the kitchen.

I lay the staff on the coffee table and settled on the sofa as he rummaged in the freezer. The apartment was elegant but compact—hardly surprising for Paris. The floor plan seemed to consist of just the living room, kitchen, and a single bedroom, which was visible through a cracked door near the TV stand. The narrow opening revealed a treadmill and the foot of what looked like a king size bed.

I ripped my gaze away as he returned with two paper plates.

"Don't tell the Parisians I fed you frozen burritos," he said, setting a steaming plate in front of me. He went back to the kitchen and returned with his own plate plus two green bottles. "The beer is French, though."

"Thanks," I said, grabbing a bottle. "After today, I think I could drink a brewery." I raised the bottle to my lips and took a healthy swig. The beer was sweet, with a touch of lemon, and I hummed with unexpected pleasure as the liquid slid down my throat.

Then I noticed Hauk was staring at me, his gaze fixed on my mouth.

I jerked the bottle down.

He seemed to rouse himself, like someone coming out of a

dream. Then he cleared his throat. "We should eat before it gets cold." He unbuckled his sword and sat in an adjacent chair.

By some unspoken agreement, we spent the next few minutes devouring our food, neither of us pausing long enough to talk. When we finished our beers, he fetched two more—and when we finished those, he grabbed a third round.

Finally, I set my empty bottle down and leaned against the sofa's armrest, a lazy buzz of contentment drifting through me. "That was perfect."

He drained the last of his beer and winked. "I *am* pretty good with a microwave."

I couldn't stifle my smile...or the tingle of awareness that rushed down my spine. No man's winks should be that sexy.

But the gesture was also a reminder of our first meeting—when he took me to his tower under the pretense of offering to train me.

I sat up straighter, my gaze falling on the staff.

He leaned forward and placed his beer on the table. "I see you found your weapon."

"Crom gave it to me."

"Along with Radegast's location."

I looked up and found him watching me with an inscrutable look on his face. "Yes."

His mouth tightened. "He liked you."

"I wouldn't say that."

Something dark flashed in his blue eyes. "When you appeared in the meadow, your face was flushed and your lips were swollen."

Anger made me bristle. "Because he kissed me without permission! And he put visions in my head. He made me feel —" I clamped my mouth shut, my face heating. Even now, faint tendrils of desire curled through me, and I could almost feel a questing tongue between my legs. I squeezed my thighs together, willing Crom out of my brain.

Hauk swore. "Gods, Elin, I'm sorry." He tensed, and his voice went gravelly. "Did he touch you?"

I shook my head. "It wasn't like that."

His shoulders relaxed, but his tone stayed rough. "It drove me nuts being stuck in that meadow, knowing you were alone with him. I tried to reach you but every time I got near the mansion I ended up right back where I started. I even tried taking it at a run, and I swear the sun got hotter just to fuck with me. I'm sorry I took you there. I should have known he'd mess with your head. Mental manipulation is his favorite trick."

"It's okay," I said, the knowledge that he'd fought so hard to rescue me doing funny things to my stomach. "I think he did it as a warning. He entered my thoughts so easily, and it felt so real..." I shuddered.

"I should have warned you about that, too. It's second nature for me to shield my thoughts, probably because I grew up in Faerie. I picture a fence or a thick wall. It gets easier with practice, and then you don't even realize you're doing it after a while."

"Crom said Radegast would read me like a book."

"Only if you're not careful. How much do you know about him?"

I thought over the stories I'd read. "Slavic god of hospitality. Loves a party. Generally merry?"

"Maybe in the past. Are you familiar with the Dyatlov Pass incident?"

My blood ran cold. "Radegast did that?"

Hauk gave a grim nod. "Nine hikers died in the Ural Mountains in the late fifties. Two of them had chest trauma caused by a force no human could have produced. Some were missing their eyes and parts of their face. The humans never figured out who killed them, but the High Fae know."

"And they let him continue killing?"

"He stopped for a while, but there have been more incidents in recent years. It's the stone. According to some in Faerie, even immortals have an innate need to know they can die. When they lose that, it makes them truly godlike. And not even a High Fae can cope with the weight of that knowledge."

I held his gaze. "Aren't you afraid that will happen to you? What if the stone drives you crazy?"

He smiled, but it didn't reach his eyes. "I don't have a lot of options. I'll still have to accept any quest that comes my way. I guess I hoped I'd stumble across a Mythical who could help me. The stone will buy me some time."

Guilt twisted through me. I needed a thousand kills before I became immortal, but at least the possibility was out there. No matter what he did, he was doomed to die.

Unless he got the Eternity Stone.

"So," he said softly, "tell me where we can find Radegast."

"I..." The knowledge lingered on my tongue—something that had to be given rather than spoken. My heart began to pound. Taking a deep breath, I stood. "I have to...touch you to pass it to you."

Surprise flared in his blue eyes, followed by an unmistakable flash of heat. When he spoke, his voice was husky. "All right. What should I do?"

I gnawed at my lip, wondering if I should ask him to stand. But no, I'd have to tip my head back for that, and I wasn't certain how the transfer was supposed to work. Maybe the location needed to slide from my mouth to his.

Finally, I skirted around the coffee table until I stood before him. "Crom put the knowledge on my tongue. So...I think I have to kiss you."

His pulse jumped in his neck. Slowly, he put his hands on the chair's armrests and eased back. "It's okay, sweetheart," he murmured. "I'll keep my hands right here the whole time. I won't move unless you tell me to. I'm not my father."

"I know that." Heart thumping, I moved between his legs, my thigh brushing one of his.

He watched me, his big body seemingly relaxed. Waiting for me to make the first move.

An unexpected thrill zipped through me. He couldn't lie. If he said he'd hold still, he'd do exactly that. By promising not to move, he'd put himself at my mercy, ceding control.

Eyes locked with his, I put my palms on his shoulders and leaned down.

He tipped his head back, his blue eyes narrowed to burning slits. His chest under my hands was solid as a rock. Leashed power—mine to take if I wished it.

I do. The thought swirled in my mind as I lowered my head and brushed his lips with mine.

He opened, but he didn't thrust his tongue against mine. Again he waited, submissive and still.

Like a lit match on gasoline, the pool of desire inside me whooshed into a fiery blaze. I climbed into his lap and deepened the kiss, thrusting my tongue against his.

He made a low, masculine sound of appreciation and opened wider, letting me all the way inside.

I took his face in my hands and slanted my mouth over his lips, my tongue plunging and stroking. He tasted of the lemony beer, wild magic, and something uniquely him—an intoxicating mix of leather and dark spices. Deep in my belly, a ribbon of desire unfurled...and spread lower. I moaned and pressed my body more firmly against his, my hips snug against the unmistakable bulge of his cock.

His chest rumbled as he answered my moan with one of his own.

As quick and unexpected as a bee sting, the coordinates for Radegast's castle shot from my tongue to his.

He jerked his head to the side, breaking contact. "Damn," he gasped, blinking in obvious pain.

"I'm sorry!" I sat back and put my fingers over my mouth. "It didn't feel that way when Crom gave them to me."

"I'm sure that was by design." He pulled my hand away from my face, then brushed his thumb over my lower lip. "I'm okay. It just startled me."

"That's...good." I licked my lips, wetting the spot he'd just touched.

His gaze dipped there. "You don't have to stop kissing me."

"Yes I do," I said, but the protest was more breath than sound. And I made no move to slide off him. I stayed where I was, the heated flesh between my legs nestled against the hard length between his.

"Lie to me," he murmured, a challenge gleaming in his gaze. "Say you don't want this as much as I do."

My gut clenched. I *was* lying to him. Every moment I didn't confess my plan for the Eternity Stone was another moment I lied. I'd accused him of pretending to help me. Now I was doing the same to him.

The only difference was I was starting to think he might not have been pretending, after all.

I slid off his lap and stood. "I don't want this."

Emotions paraded across his face. There was surprise, followed by a flare of anger, and then finally cold resignation. He rose, and I backed around the table, putting space between us.

An uncomfortable silence reigned. Then he gathered his sword and cloak. "I'll sleep on the sofa. You can have the bed."

"I'm fine out here." The was no way I was spending the night on sheets that smelled of him.

He sighed. "I have one bathroom, Elin, and it's *inside* my bedroom. It'll be a lot easier if you take the bed."

I lifted my chin. "I said I'm fine. I'll shower in the morning." As much as I wanted to have a long, intimate encounter with hot water, my nerves were too raw to go through the motions of regular house guest stuff. He'd have to fetch me a change of clothes and show me where he kept the towels. How could I do that when the taste of his kiss lingered on my tongue?

"There are blankets in the closet by the front door," he said finally. Then he turned and walked to the bedroom. Just before he crossed the threshold, he stopped and spoke over his shoulder. "I promised I'd be honest with you or be forsworn. So here are two things I know to be true. I've never wanted a woman as much as I want you."

I stood frozen, my heart pounding.

"And I've never seen anyone lie as badly as you did just now."

CHAPTER

FIFTEEN

About a half hour after Hauk disappeared into his bedroom, my bladder let me know how stupid I'd been to decline the use of his bathroom.

For a while, I tried to ignore it. I lay on the sofa with a blanket pulled to my chin, my mind on the dangerous quest that lay ahead of me.

But it was no use. The three beers I'd had at dinner weren't going anywhere.

Gritting my teeth, I threw off the blanket and hobbled to Hauk's door. I stood there a minute, embarrassment and indecision gnawing at me.

This is ridiculous. Steeling myself, I rapped my knuckles on the door. "Hauk?"

No answer.

He was probably already sleeping. He'd spent hours in the blazing sun in Faerie.

I knocked harder...then knocked again.

The room was quiet as a tomb.

My bladder spasmed, going from uncomfortable to painful.

Cursing under my breath, I turned the knob and opened the door a couple inches. Immediately, steam wafted around me and the soft hiss of a running shower hit my ears. The bedroom was dark save for a soft glow coming from the bathroom, which was visible through an open door.

And a nude Hauk stood in a glass shower, his head bent and his large body in profile as he stroked his fist up and down the biggest cock I'd ever seen.

My breath hitched. Heat prickled over my skin.

He faced the showerhead, one hand braced on the tiled wall. Water pounded over a physique that belonged on Mount Olympus. His hair hung over one broad shoulder, the golden ends dripping water. His brow was furrowed, his sexy mouth parted as he gasped low, panting breaths.

My gaze traveled lower, instant heat rushing to my center. His bicep bunched and flexed as he pumped his heavy shaft with its thick, veined length and bulbous head. As he moved, his ass flexed, the taut muscle making my mouth water.

He moaned, and I jerked my eyes up, a gasp lodged in my throat.

He'd tipped his head back, and his hand worked faster, his knuckles white as his fisted his shaft in a grip so tight it looked painful.

I should go. It was wrong—so, so wrong—to watch him this way. But my feet wouldn't move. I couldn't tear my gaze off the blistering scene unfolding before me. My heart pumped harder, the beat echoing between my legs as I grew wetter. Needier. My nipples tightened, and my eyes drifted over his hand and down his ass to his legs.

His thighs were thick and round as tree trunks, his calves long and lean. Even his feet were well-formed and sexy, his toes gripping the tile as he fucked his hand.

Water cascaded down his body, little rivulets and tributaries running over his tanned, muscled skin. The tendons in his forearm tightened as he stroked himself, his heavy sac swaying between his legs.

He was magnificent—a warrior in his prime with a body built to conquer and claim.

And gods help me, I wanted him to conquer me.

My cheeks blazed. Hot moisture gathered between my legs, the flesh there aching.

He picked up the pace.

My heart sped up, matching it, until it beat in sync with his fist.

Up and down. Harder and faster. He pumped himself, the big muscles in his back bunching, his body a machine of muscle, sinew, and smooth skin.

My lips parted, my breaths coming in gasps. A moan hovered in my throat.

Steam wafted around his glistening cock and flying fist. His ass jerked, the muscles firing as he thrust his hips.

My sex clenched. I bit back a whimper. Something—some sixth sense—made me shift my gaze up.

He stared at me, his blue eyes glittering with lust and triumph.

He'd caught me—and he had no intention of stopping.

Or letting me go.

He continued working his shaft, but now he held my gaze captive. Held my body in place with the weight of his stare.

Moisture seeped from my sex. I took my lower lip between my teeth, biting back the moan pushing against my throat.

Lightning forked across his irises, the tiny flashes flickering silver across the blue.

I let out a shuddering breath. An urge to rock my hips back and forth overwhelmed me.

He dipped his gaze to my mouth. His movements became

jerkier, his elbow pistoning up and down. Then he seized my gaze again and held it. His expression was fierce, almost defiant. His shoulders jerked once, twice, then he threw his head back on a shout. He squeezed his eyes shut, his mouth open as his release pumped from his cock. It went on in an endless stream, thick jets striking the tile in lashes I could almost feel on my skin.

My pulse throbbed in my neck. Sweat dampened my hairline. Suddenly, the bedroom was uncomfortably hot. Steam swirled around me, carrying the scent of soap and man.

Hauk turned his head and opened his eyes, his gaze locked with mine. Slowly, he gripped his shaft and ran his fist down his length one last time, squeezing the last drops of come from the tip. His lips moved, and I didn't need sound to understand the words he mouthed.

Lie to me.

My sex clenched.

The room was close...the air too hot.

I whirled and rushed to the living room. With shaking hands, I flung back the curtains and slid the heavy glass door aside. With a sob, I stumbled into the cold Parisian night.

CHAPTER
SIXTEEN

ap, tap, tap.

I jerked awake with a gasp. My breath fogged in front of my face. Straight ahead, the Eiffel Tower blazed gold against a black sky. Beneath it, the sprawl of buildings and roads were dark and quiet. Paris was asleep. I had been, too—until now. I pushed myself out of the metal chair I'd settled in for the night. As I straightened, a lancing pain shot through my bladder.

Tap, tap, tap.

I spun around, my heart racing.

Asher stood inside the apartment with the staff in his hand. His green eyes twinkled as he spoke through the glass. "You called?"

I scrambled around the chair. He slid the glass open and caught me as I rushed into his arms.

"Where were you?" I croaked, inhaling his scent of wind and leaves. "I tried to contact you through the door but you never came."

"I'm so sorry, Elin," he murmured. "My guess is Harald shut it down somehow. He knew you would ask me for help."

I lifted my head. "I hate him," I said hotly.

"You have every right to." Asher's eyes fired with anger. "He betrays my sister's memory by treating his own child this way."

I drew a shuddering breath. "If he comes near me again, I'll kill him." As I spoke the words, the rightness of them flowed through me.

Asher lifted the staff. "With this on your side, I don't doubt it. Where'd you get such a beauty?"

"Hauk gave it to me."

A knowing look entered his eyes. "The Chris Hemsworth lookalike snoring in the other room?"

"He's the Hersir of Bjørneskalle. I...kind of agreed to go on a quest with him."

"Ah." Asher stepped back. "Come inside and tell me everything."

I darted an anxious glance over his shoulder. "What if he wakes up?"

"I'm not without tricks, niece of mine."

Hope soared in my chest. "Can you keep him asleep while I use the bathroom?"

"Yes, but I can't promise not to ogle him while you do your business."

I raised an eyebrow. "I didn't think men were your cup of tea."

"Elin, that man is the whole teapot." He jerked his head toward the bedroom. "Now go. Your eyes are turning yellow."

~

Once I'd relieved my aching bladder, Asher and I settled on the sofa.

He sat cross-legged with the staff lengthwise over his knees, petting the polished wood like someone might caress a cat. "So it formed into a spear without you asking it to?"

I nodded. "And it set the death nettles on Maya. At least I think it did. It seems to have a mind of its own."

"Mmmm. Most things from Faerie do."

"Do you think it's dangerous?"

He tilted his head. "Power is power. Like a hurricane or a tornado. Those things are neither good nor evil. They just *are*. Wild energy can be beautiful...and deadly." He gave me a look that was both loving and slightly censuring. "You've ignored your nymph side too long. I keep telling you there's more to it than sex."

I could hardly argue when everything he said was true. He'd always encouraged me to embrace whatever little magic I'd inherited from my mother, and I'd resisted at every turn.

A memory of the naiads from Crom's fountain flashed in my head. They'd seemed so...*brainless* as they danced nude in the water. *Flighty*—the word Harald had loved to use whenever I did something too unseemly for a berserker.

But maybe I should have taken a closer look.

Asher smoothed his palm down the staff. "So. You're on a quest to help Hauk get his immortality."

"Yes." I couldn't tell him about my mother. She'd been his only sibling, and no brother and sister had ever been closer. But he was also a creature of Faerie, and I knew without asking that he wouldn't approve of me using a powerful Fae artifact to bring someone back from the dead. The High Fae wanted the stone returned. Asher would never risk angering them. If he learned of my plan, he'd try to stop me.

I cleared my throat. "Yes, that's what I'm doing."

"But you have feelings for him."

I shook my head. "He needs a nymph. I need to get away from Harald. End of story."

Asher didn't look impressed. "So he's in the bedroom and you're sleeping on the freezing balcony? That's a high-grade lovers' quarrel right there."

"We're not lovers," I huffed.

"No," he said, his tone amused. "Not yet, anyway. But you want each other."

"You're making assumptions."

He gestured at himself. "Satyr, remember? I know how dumb people can be about sex. And the two of you are being awfully dumb. I'm no warrior, but it seems dangerous to take on a High Fae like Radegast when you're this distracted."

"What are you suggesting? That I should just sleep with him?" There was no point keeping up the pretense that all was innocent between Hauk and me. Asher was too observant to be fooled.

He shrugged. "You've got an itch. So scratch it."

"That is absolutely the worst phrasing you could have used in this context."

"I'm just saying you shouldn't deny what's in front of you." He flicked his gaze toward the bedroom door. "Or in the other room."

Maybe not. But Hauk was going to *hate* me once he found out I'd lied.

Asher leaned forward. "We live a long time, Elin. But no one is guaranteed anything." His gaze softened, and I wondered if he was thinking of my mother. "You worry about how others perceive you. It's not easy being a half-breed, especially when you're not entirely thrilled with one of your halves."

"I never said—"

He held up a hand. "It's understandable. But nymphs and satyrs aren't without power. Our magic comes directly from the earth itself. It's raw, wild energy—the kind that makes passion pump through your veins. It's not a sword, but it can be a weapon under the right circumstances. Maybe you should try embracing it." He lay his hand on the staff.

And lowered his glamour.

His skin grew darker, his hair a riot of unruly curls around his head. The rich, dark mass was threaded with leaves. His green eyes glowed, and the angles of his face became sharper. His ears tapered up to delicate points, and something that looked like moss covered part of his neck. The swirling blue tattoos were the same, but now they appeared to move, the patterns shifting and rearranging themselves.

My Uncle Asher was still there, but now he was something more. Something beautiful and wild and maybe a little dangerous. Out of nowhere, a rush of warm air swept the room. For a moment, the sun filled the apartment, splashing cheerful yellow light over everything. Birds sang, their notes high and pure. The smell of honeysuckle and pine filled my lungs.

I wanted to tip my head back and let the rays warm my skin. To sprint through the forest, leaves crunching under my bare feet. I wanted to trail my fingers over the tops of flowers as I waded through tall grass.

I wanted to *feel*.

Asher lifted his hand from the staff.

The sun and wind disappeared.

His glamour snapped back into place.

"Bend without breaking, Elin," he said gently. "But first you have to bend."

CHAPTER

SEVENTEEN

"Are you sure those fit okay?"

I jumped at the sound of Hauk's voice. He pointed to my boots, which I'd just finished lacing. "Yes," I said.

He grunted and stuffed a spare set of gloves in his pack.

I chewed the inside of my cheek. He'd apparently decided we were going to pretend last night hadn't happened.

Unfortunately, I hadn't stopped thinking about it.

After Asher left, I'd gotten a few hours of fitful sleep on the sofa, my mind spinning with images from the shower—and the dishonesty that hung around my neck like a weight.

I'd been so preoccupied, I hadn't given any thought to Radegast or the quest.

Around dawn, Hauk had emerged from his bedroom and set about making pancakes. He'd made no mention of the shower. He'd hardly looked at me as he moved around the apartment with brisk efficiency.

"Bathroom is yours," he'd said, his back to me while he poured batter onto a griddle. "I left clothes for you on the bed."

Breakfast would have been a perfect opportunity to clear the air. Instead, he'd placed a heaping stack of pancakes in front of me and proceeded to load our packs with supplies while I ate.

So we hadn't talked about the night before—and now I wasn't certain how to handle myself around him. Was he angry I'd watched him?

Upset I hadn't joined him?

At that thought, a rush of heat swept my skin. The invitation had been there in his eyes.

"I don't think they're tight enough," he said suddenly, standing and coming to where I stood by the coffee table. He knelt and undid my laces, his long fingers working quickly. "You'll get blisters if they're too loose."

I gazed down at his head as more heat spread through me. He was dressed head to toe in black cold weather gear, and his dark blond hair was a striking contrast to his dark sweater. As he retied my laces, I couldn't tear my eyes off his hands.

He'd gripped his length so hard, those same fingers wrapped around his thick shaft...

"I'm sure they're fine," I said hoarsely.

He stilled, then lifted his gaze.

For the first time all morning, our eyes met.

Held.

And the naked, unguarded desire in his gaze seared my skin.

Awareness rocketed through me. He wasn't indifferent about last night, I realized.

He was holding himself back.

Slowly, he rose to his full height, reversing the angle so now he looked down at me. "I'm worried about you," he murmured. "The snow is deep in the Urals, and Radegast is known to set traps around his castles."

My heart thumped. "I'll be okay. I've got all the gear I need." The extreme weather clothing he'd given me was top of the line—long underwear, fur-lined boots, waterproof pants, and a thick jacket. "Where did you get it all?"

His eyes grew shuttered. "I bought it last week. I wasn't sure you'd agree to come with me, but I...hoped."

Because he'd needed a nymph.

But the connection between us was real. I couldn't deny it anymore. Not after last night.

The weight of dishonesty tugged harder. I'd tucked my mother's mirror in my back pocket, and the metal seemed to burn through the fabric of my pants and press against my skin like an accusation. "Hauk—"

"You don't have to do this, Elin. I'll carry out the quest on my own. And it won't change the way I feel about you." He brushed a lock of hair off my shoulder. "We'll pick up where we left off when I get back."

It won't change the way I feel about you. He couldn't lie. He'd taken a vow to always tell me the truth.

I swallowed the rest of my sentence. If I confessed now, it would ruin everything. And he'd try to take down Radegast by himself. "I can't let you go alone," I said, misery and desire twining around each other in my chest. "You need me. And...I want to help you." It was the truth. I wanted to help him escape Crom's curse.

I just wanted to bring my mother back, too.

But I couldn't do both.

He gazed at me steadily, oblivious to the tug of war in my head. "Then let's make this quest count. Give me your hand."

I placed my palm face-up in his.

He pulled out a pocketknife and flicked it open. "Have you taken a blood oath before?"

"No." My stomach fluttered. "But I know the words."

"Fingers straight. I'll make it quick."

I forced myself to watch.

The knife flashed, and fire licked over my palm.

I clenched my jaw against the burn as a line of red appeared on my skin.

He gave a throaty growl of approval and released my hand.

I licked my palm, tasting copper. "Odin the All-Father, lord of wisdom and death, I undertake this quest in your name. May your hand guide me as I seek to bring justice to one who deserves it."

Heat flared in Hauk's eyes as I lowered my throbbing hand to my side. Our breaths mingled, and then he bent his head and kissed me, tasting my bloody oath. It was dark and forbidden, and my panties dampened as lust snaked a hot path through my core.

He lifted his head and stared at me with eyes gone silver. "Soon."

I gave a shaky nod. Whatever happened, our coming together was a certainty.

He went to his pack and swung it onto his back with ease. Then he brought mine over and helped me do the same. He handed me the staff and extended a hand toward the center of the room.

The air rippled, the Eiffel Tower outside the window going blurry.

He threaded the fingers of his free hand through mine. "Ready?"

I nodded. "Ready."

We stepped into the portal.

WIND RUSHED BY MY HEAD, AND WHITE FILLED MY VISION. FRIGID AIR blasted my face. I'd landed in the middle of a blizzard.

Alone.

Panic rocked me. "Hauk!" I flung out my arms. What if I'd lost him? Or stumbled into the wrong plane? I might never find my way back.

"Elin!" Something seized my shoulders. Then his face appeared in front of mine.

Relief made my knees weak. I raised my voice over the wind. "How do we get out of this?"

"We don't!" he shouted. "We're here."

My stomach clenched. "This is it?"

"These are the coordinates." He looked around—or at least I thought he did. It was hard to tell with so much snow flying.

He turned back to me. "Grab my jacket and don't let go."

I took a fistful of material and tugged to let him know I'd complied.

He walked forward, pulling me after him. Wind screamed in my ears, and snow quickly clumped on my eyelashes. Each breath burned a white-hot path from my sinuses to my chest. We went at a snail's pace, sinking to our hips with every step. At first, I tried to use the staff to propel me forward, but the wood sank so deep I had to fight to pry it loose over and over again. Eventually, Hauk took it from me and fastened it across the top of his pack.

We went on like that for hours. My teeth chattered—then I grew so cold my jaw seemed to freeze in place. Hauk was my only point of reference in a sea of endless white. His pack swayed ahead of me, his broad shoulders a steady, reliable constant in the frozen wasteland.

My world shrank to the black outline of his body, the frigid air burning my lungs, and the crunch of my plodding footsteps in the snow. The terrain didn't vary at all. There were no hills or inclines. No rocks or landmarks. Not even an occasional tree root. It was just a flat expanse of relentless white.

The muscles in my legs burned...and then the pain faded to numbness.

And I grew warm. It was the comforting glow of a few shots of whiskey. The warmth started in my belly and then spread to my arms and legs. It carried me—and tempted me. Like a thick, fluffy blanket, it wanted to wrap me up and settle me on the ground.

Because if I could just close my eyes, I could *really* get comfortable.

Hauk kept walking, his boots punching through the snow. A spark of irritation fired inside me. How could I curl up and sleep when he kept slogging us forward?

I tried to release his jacket, but my fingers wouldn't unclench.

I tugged.

He kept going.

The warmth beckoned. *If I could just sleep for a couple minutes...*

Hauk continued moving forward.

My irritation grew.

I sank to my knees, not caring whether he dragged me. It didn't matter. The snow was soft.

"Elin..." Someone was calling me. Hands touched my face. I brushed them away.

"Too tired," I mumbled. Or maybe I just thought it. My lips were too heavy to move.

Then I was up and swinging through the air. I landed against something solid and warm.

Yes. Heat was good. A sigh of contentment slid through my frozen lips.

My body rocked back and forth—a gentle swaying that

promised sleep and a respite from the wind that ripped at my hair and clothes.

I snuggled against the warmth. Black covered my vision, and it was a welcome change from the blinding white.

The swaying continued.

After a while, my heart rate matched its pace.

I sighed again and let the blackness swallow me.

CHAPTER
EIGHTEEN

I woke on my back with a stone ceiling over my head. A thick blanket covered me, and something soft supported my head. A short distance away, a small fire crackled and leapt.

For a moment, I lay there, listless and disoriented, a heavy weight tugging at my eyelids.

The fire was warm against my face. So much better than the brutal sting of snow.

Snow.

My eyes shot wide as everything rushed back.

"Elin!" There was a shuffle of bare feet and then Hauk was at my side, his face a mask of worry. He wore nothing but his body-hugging cold weather tights and long-sleeved shirt, and his hair was wet and tied back from his face in a knot. He put a hand on my forehead. "How do you feel?"

"Good," I murmured. I shifted experimentally—and realized I was naked under the blanket.

And I didn't have my mother's mirror.

I bolted upright, my heart pounding. "Where are my clothes?"

"Drying, but—" He cut himself off as I scrambled to my feet, letting the blanket fall. "Elin, what are you—"

My clothes were spread on the ground on the other side of the fire. Ignoring Hauk's protests, I darted around the blaze and rushed to my pants. Crouching, I patted the pockets.

It was there—hard and round. Hands shaking, I pulled the mirror out and cracked it open.

The glass was intact.

My breath left me in a rush, my relief so intense I felt lightheaded.

Hauk's palm touched my bare back. "Something important to you?" he murmured.

I turned my head as he knelt beside me. "It was my mother's," I said thickly. "I thought"—I swallowed—"maybe I'd lost it."

Lost her.

She was so vulnerable in the mirror. So breakable.

He offered a soft smile, the firelight flickering in his deep blue eyes. "But everything's all right?"

My heart squeezed as a decision took root in my chest.

"Yes," I lied, my voice barely above a whisper. "Everything is all right."

His gaze dropped to my mouth.

And the air shifted. It swelled and stretched, throbbing as if it had a pulse.

Something primal swirled around us. Unruly and wild.

I waited, my heart beginning to pound. *Lie to me*, he'd said. And I had. And I would again—until my fingers closed around the stone and I brought my mother back to life.

But I wouldn't lie to him about *this*—the crackling energy

between us. I couldn't give him the truth with my lips, but I could give it to him with my body.

And hopefully, when the time came, it would be enough.

Holding his gaze, I rose to my feet. I shook my hair back from my face and stood bare before him. The air danced over my skin, pebbling my nipples and teasing the wetness already creeping between my thighs.

Slowly, he stood, his big body unfolding. He was menacing in all black—his clothes straining against muscles honed by killing monsters and villains. He looked me over in a slow sweep, his eyes burning a path from my mouth to the damp folds between my thighs.

Heat blistered over my skin. The wild energy in the air flowed faster.

I breathed it in, letting it fill my lungs.

Honeysuckle and roses teased my nose. The energy spread through me, heating my blood.

I cupped my breasts, which felt heavy and swollen. "I want you," I told him. "I want your tongue on me and your cock inside me."

He was on me in a heartbeat, lifting me and carrying me around the fire. He tumbled me down on the bed of blankets and flipped me onto my hands and knees. He knelt behind me and cupped my pussy. "You want my tongue on you?" he asked, his voice nothing more than a growl.

"Yes," I groaned, thrusting my ass back at him. I looked over my shoulder, catching him ripping his shirt over his head and yanking off his pants. When he was naked, he put a firm hand between my shoulder blades and pressed me down.

My nipples brushed the soft blanket, and I moaned and bowed my spine.

He slid a long, thick finger into my wetness. "Wider," he barked.

The command sizzled over my skin, concentrating around my clit as I pressed my cheek into the blankets and moved my knees apart.

He withdrew his finger and his palms landed hard on my ass—not quite a slap, but close. Growling low in his throat, he squeezed my cheeks and pressed me open. Air caressed my heated flesh and puckered hole, and then his tongue delved where his finger had been a second before.

I moaned and sank deeper, lifting my ass high. Seeking his wicked tongue.

He plunged again, spearing my entrance in swift, thorough strokes before licking his way down my folds to suckle my clit.

My fingers dug into the blankets, and I became a wild thing, writhing and shoving my hips back. He grasped my hips and held me in an iron grip as he licked and sucked, working his tongue over my throbbing center. He scraped his teeth over the sensitive bud, then soothed the sting with a firm swipe of his tongue. His palms pressed me wider, his thumb dipping into my asshole as he sucked me hard. Just as my body began to fly apart, he pulled away and flipped me onto my back.

I arched, wanton and restless, my thighs falling wide.

"So wet," he growled, rising onto his knees. He swiped a callused palm over my sex and spread my juices over his cock.

I moaned, growing even wetter at the sight of my glistening desire coating his shaft. My mouth watered with the need to taste him, to kneel at his feet and suck him down my throat.

There was power in that. I realized it now. Sex could be a weapon, but it could also be a gift. Either way, it was powerful. I'd wasted so much time being afraid of it.

He pumped himself, aided by my wetness. His magnificent cock was thick and ready, a bead of moisture clinging to the tip.

But he didn't give it to me. Instead, he fixed his smoldering gaze between my legs. "Show me where you want me."

I lifted my knees and dipped two fingers into my pussy, stroking in and out. I was so wet the sounds drowned out the crackling fire. "Here," I gasped. "Please."

"Where else?"

I drew my fingers to my clit and rubbed in tight circles, shivering as sparks danced across my skin. "Here..." I moaned. "Everywhere."

His eyes were fully silver. The light from the fire painted him in shades of gold, turning him into a bronzed god. Scars decorated his chest and stomach—evidence of long-ago battles and quests. He continued stroking his cock, his thick thighs spread and his hips pumping in a languid rhythm.

"Do you want inside me?" I asked, turning the tables. I dragged my fingers down my sodden lips and circled my entrance, stirring my wetness in lazy circles.

He clenched his jaw. "You have no fucking idea," he ground out.

I dipped my other hand between my legs, then carried both hands to my breasts. I plucked at my nipples, painting the tips with my juices so they glistened in the firelight. I arched my back, thrusting my breasts toward the cave's ceiling as I spread my legs wider. "I bet you want to plunge deep," I said, my voice breathless. "You want to take that big cock and bury it in my—"

He surged forward with a growl and pinned my arms above my head. His chest smashed my breasts and his cock prodded my sex. He dropped his face to my neck and touched his tongue to my pulse, my jaw, the hollow of my throat. "I'll bury it everywhere," he muttered in a voice like gravel. He bit the skin over the throbbing vein in my neck. "Your mouth," he rasped.

"Your sopping pussy and that tight little ass you waved in my face."

I groaned, my eyes fluttering shut.

"Ah," he said knowingly, "you like that idea, don't you, Elin? I'll put you on your knees and order you to spread yourself open for me. Then I'll slick your hole and give you my fingers. And if you're a very good girl, I'll put my cock between your plump cheeks and ream your pretty asshole until you forget everything but my name."

"Yes," I gasped, heat singeing my veins.

"But not tonight," he murmured, his lips brushing mine. "Tonight is for this." He transferred my wrists to one hand, gripped himself, and shoved inside me in one swift thrust.

My cry merged with his moan of pleasure. I dug my heels into the blankets and thrust my hips higher, taking him even deeper. Grinding my clit against the top of his shaft.

"So greedy," he said on a chuckle. He pinched my nipple as he began to move, rolling his hips so he brushed my clit on every thrust. "Such a hungry, wet pussy begging for my cock."

"More," I groaned, flinging my legs wide. With my hands pinned and his weight holding me down, I could only receive him. Was helpless to do anything but take what he gave me. It was quick and rough and so perfect I cried out again.

He gripped one of my legs behind my knee and pushed it up by my chest, opening me wide. Thrusting harder, he gazed down our bodies to where he entered me, his shaft spearing me ruthlessly. Showing no mercy.

It was exactly what I wanted. To be taken and claimed. For him to stamp himself all over me.

He dragged his eyes back up my body, over my quivering stomach and bouncing breasts. When he reached my face, he gave me a look so dark and possessive I forgot how to breathe.

He shifted position, bracing his weight on his forearms on either side of my head.

Then he fucked in earnest.

He fell into a pounding rhythm, his thrusts so powerful my back inched across the blankets. I wrapped my legs around him and dug my fingers into his shoulders.

"Yes!" I gasped.

"Hold on," he growled. "Going to give you every... last...drop."

"Please." I needed it so badly.

He cursed and thrust faster.

Then neither of us said anything at all, our words reduced to pleasured groans and panting breaths. Sweat slicked our skin. His hips slapped against mine. The fire danced higher, and the heat in my veins burned hotter. I rushed toward the edge.

And fell over it, spinning into nothing and everything. My mind emptied of worries and cares as I squeezed my legs around his hips and threw my head back, my orgasm blasting me apart.

He was right behind me, plunging deep and coming on a shout.

We finished together, our bodies going slack. He collapsed on top of me, then rolled us to the side with his cock still buried deep. For a moment, I drifted in a blissful haze, his heart thumping against my back.

He spoke at last, his voice thick and sated. "That was even better than I'd dreamed."

I turned in his arms, and our eyes met. "You dreamed about it?"

His lips curved. "Only every minute of every day." He kissed my forehead, his breath stirring my hair. "The only thing I'll be thinking about tomorrow is killing Radegast as quickly as possible so we can do it again."

My gut clenched. He was already thinking about tomorrow...and the next day, and the day after that. He thought we had a future together.

But in a few hours, I was going to blow it all up.

CHAPTER
NINETEEN

Hauk's voice reached me across the snow. "You okay?"

I stuck the tip of the staff in the ground and squinted against the bright morning sun. He'd stopped several paces ahead and stood looking at me over his shoulder. A rope stretched between us, the ends clipped to each of our belts. *"In case you fall or pass out,"* he'd explained before we left the cave. *"This way, I won't drag you like yesterday."*

I *hated* the Ural Mountains.

I spit hair out of my mouth. "Yes. How much farther?" I probably sounded like a child pestering their parents on a road trip. Although the blizzard was gone, the terrain was still the same flat, endless white from yesterday. We'd been walking for hours, and the protein bars we had for breakfast were a distant memory. My thighs burned and a headache brewed in my temples.

He pointed. "There."

In the distance, the top of a castle turret peeked over a line of evergreens.

Relief and apprehension mixed in my gut. Our journey might be wrapping up, but Radegast waited at the end of it.

Hauk gave the rope a gentle tug. "Let's go."

As we neared the forest, an unsettled feeling crept over me. The trees were tall and ancient-looking, with thick roots that crawled over the ground.

And there were no sounds—not even bird chatter. It was so quiet I could hear the blood rushing in my ears.

As we moved deeper, I gripped the staff more tightly. "This isn't normal."

"It's a spell," Hauk muttered, unclipping the rope that connected us. "Radegast layers enchantments around his dwellings. The blizzard was an outer band that probably prevents most humans from wandering too close." He swept a gaze around the trees that soared over us. "Let's keep moving."

We continued walking, our boots crunching over fallen leaves instead of snow. The air grew thicker...and warmer. After another few minutes, Hauk stopped and shrugged out of his coat. Together, we stripped down to our boots, pants, and tight-fitting long-sleeved shirts. The material was supposed to be moisture-wicking, but sweat still dampened my back.

"We'll leave the packs," he said, leaning them against a tree. "I never intended to take them the whole way." He knelt and pulled his tattered brown cloak from a front pocket.

"You're wearing that?" I asked.

He swung it around his shoulders, then pulled the hood over his head. Immediately, his features became indistinct. Forgettable. He lowered the hood, and his face was recognizable once more. "It's enchanted. Humans don't see me at all and Mythicals see me as boring and uninteresting. It's the only way I'll get close to Radegast without him realizing what I am."

"I wish I had one," I said.

He came to me and clasped my upper arms. "You don't need it. When I say he's a sucker for nymphs, I mean it. Just..."

I raised an eyebrow. "Act like a bimbo?"

Regret flashed in his gaze. "I didn't mean—"

"It's all right." I lifted onto my toes and brushed my lips over his. "Sex can be a weapon under the right circumstances."

His eyes flickered between blue and silver. "Well, you've definitely conquered me."

We stared at each other, heat arcing between us. Then he took a step back. "We should keep going before it gets dark."

The reminder of our surroundings was enough to cool my desire. "Okay."

He led us deeper into the forest, helping me over the roots, which grew larger and more twisted. The tree canopy blotted out the sun, plunging us into anemic gray light. My palm holding the staff grew sweaty, and I had to keep wiping it on my pants.

Eventually, Hauk stopped and cursed. "I feel like I've seen the same stump twenty times."

I stared, and my heart beat faster. "You're right." But it wasn't just any tree stump.

It was my mother's. The one she sat on when I spoke to her in the mirror. I'd recognize it anywhere. As the realization spread through me, the mirror in my back pocket grew warm.

And then hot.

"Here." I thrust the staff at Hauk and dug in my pocket.

His brow furrowed, but he stayed silent as I pulled out the mirror and opened it.

My mother stood in the forest—and now I recognized it as the same forest Hauk and I stood in. Her simple white dress puddled on the ground. Vines wove in and out of her reddish curls.

"Elin!" She clasped her hands in front of her, but she didn't smile. And for a second, her green eyes seemed to shift to Hauk.

But that couldn't be right. The enchantment was for me alone.

Behind her, wind picked up. Leaves swept around her feet. She looked over her shoulder, as if she was startled by a noise.

"Mom?" I gripped the mirror until my hand hurt.

In the mirror, the sun dimmed. Behind her, lightning flashed. A second later, thunder boomed.

What is happening?

She faced me, her features pinched and her voice tight. "He approaches, Elin. You have a choice to make."

"Radegast?"

More lightning. Her eyes widened, and she looked behind her again. When she swung back, she spoke in an anxious rush. "Doors will be closed to you, my daughter. You must make your own."

"What?" I shouted into the mirror. "What do you mean?"

She began chanting. The words were the same as her usual song, but her voice was low and terrible, like a witch invoking a spell.

Ash and oak and willow, three
Which one shall my dearest be?

Her eyes glowed, the green glittering like emeralds.

Oh, ash with leaves the first to fall
And ancient oak, its branches tall

The fine hairs on my arms lifted. A feeling of dread bore down on me.

Still willow weeps for Babylon
And forgotten times once here, now gone
Each one so very dear to me

She tipped her head back and raised her voice.

YET ASH WITH FRUIT THAT HOLDS THE KEY

As the last word echoed, she stepped back and tossed something into the air. Small and gold, it flipped end over end.

And into the air in front of me.

I stumbled back.

Hauk reached out and snatched the object before it could fall.

"What is it?" I gasped, my heart in my throat.

He opened his hand. A small, golden skeleton key lay on his palm.

I looked in the mirror, but my mother was gone, the stump deserted in the empty forest. Words spilled from me in a babble. "She never does that. The mirror is spelled. She's supposed to be like a recording that plays the same thing over and over. Did you see her face? I think someone is trying to hurt her."

Hauk looked at the key in his hand, then lifted a cautious gaze to mine. "How could someone hurt her?" he asked gently. "I thought she'd passed away."

"She...did." Didn't she?

His cast a wary look around. "This is Radegast's doing. Another enchantment."

The ground rumbled. We both jumped, and Hauk moved even closer to me. A golden line appeared on a tree trunk next to the stump. It blazed like fire, then lengthened as though drawn by an invisible hand.

"It's an ash tree," I breathed. "Just like in her song."

He passed me the staff. "Take this. And be ready for anything."

The golden line continued up the ash trunk, trailing tiny sparks like some unseen metalsmith was soldering it into the wood. It blazed a path up, then made an abrupt right angle and went in a straight light. After a short distance, it made another right angle and trailed down. When it reached the base of the trunk it sputtered out, leaving a perfect golden rectangle.

"It's a door," Hauk murmured.

I looked at him. "And we have a key."

He flipped his hood up and drew his sword. "Stay behind me."

"I already planned to."

He flashed a quick grin and went to the tree. The "knob" was a small circle burned into the bark. Beneath it was an obvious keyhole. He inserted my mother's key.

Click.

There was another rumble, and then the "door" swung inward.

He lifted his sword, his knees slightly bent. When nothing came barreling toward us, some of the tension left his shoulders. Without taking his eyes off the opening, he spoke in a low voice. "I'm going in. You stay on my ass, all right? Just like in Faerie."

"All right."

He led us through the door and into a long, stone hallway lit with torches. Just inside, he stopped and looked around. His gaze went grim. "I know this place. It's *Nochnaya Krepost*. The Night Fortress. Radegast's main dwelling."

"Are we in Faerie?" I whispered.

"No. We would have felt it if we'd passed through a portal. But this place is so heavily spelled it's invisible to humans. Radegast moves the entrances around to keep the other High Fae from finding him."

My mother's voice echoed through my head. *Doors will be closed to you, my daughter. You must make your own.*

My heart squeezed. If Radegast was trying to trick us, using my mother was an effective way to do it. For the first time in my life, I'd had a real conversation with her. It was hard to believe it was highly deceptive magic.

And that was what made it so dangerous.

"What do we do now?" I asked Hauk.

He grasped my chin with gentle fingers and guided my lips to his for a quick, chaste kiss. "We walk," he said, his blue eyes steady. "And we finish our quest and go home."

Guilt lanced me. Radegast's enchantments had given me a glimpse of what it would be like to have my mother in my life. How could I pass up a chance to use the stone?

But how could I keep lying to Hauk when I couldn't deny the connection between us anymore?

I licked my lips, tasting his kiss.

"Hauk," I said suddenly. "There something I need to—"

"We have a strict guest list here," a nasty voice called out.

Hauk whirled, sword in hand, and shoved me behind him.

A stout, childlike figure stood a short distance away, its beady eyes narrowed and cold. "And you two are most definitely not on it."

CHAPTER
TWENTY

The figure glared at us with unconcealed malice. It was clearly some kind of Fae with its tiny body and inhuman features. Its looks were androgynous, but I got the impression it was male. A shock of red hair stood up from its head like a swirl of cotton candy. Its ears tapered to points.

It grinned, revealing multiple rows of sharp-looking teeth. "I'm going to enjoy killing you."

I stepped around Hauk. "I-I'm a nymph. We came to see Radegast."

The creature looked me up and down. "You don't look like a nymph."

"She is," Hauk said. "We heard your master welcomes them at his banquets."

The beady eyes focused on my staff. Then the creature lifted its nose and sniffed. "You don't smell like a nymph."

"We've been traveling," I said. "It was a long journey to get here." My pulse raced. "I'm anxious to meet your master." I dropped my voice, trying for a sultry purr. "I've heard so much about him."

Silence stretched. The torches sputtered and hissed. I held my breath, ready to swing the staff if the creature attacked.

"All right," it said at last, "but you'll leave your weapons here."

I tensed, ready to argue.

"That's fine," Hauk said. He crouched and placed his sword on the ground.

The creature gave me an expectant look.

Reluctance tugged at me. The staff hadn't demonstrated any magical properties on the long journey to Radegast's domain, but I'd grown used to its weight in my hand. Concealing a grimace, I lay it on the ground next to Hauk's sword.

"Follow me," the creature said. It swiveled and marched down the hallway.

My breath spilled from me in a relieved rush. I exchanged an anxious look with Hauk, and we fell into step behind the Fae.

For someone so small, he moved quickly, and I found myself lengthening my strides to keep up. We walked so swiftly I didn't have time to think about strategy or what would happen when we reached our destination. After a few minutes of the breakneck pace, a pair of thick wooden doors loomed ahead.

The Fae pushed them wide, revealing a great hall straight out of a medieval castle. Colorful banners hung from the walls and a raised dais held a long table covered in a richly embroidered tablecloth. The table groaned with serving platters piled with food.

Next to the dais stood a massive throne.

And it was occupied by the biggest male I'd ever seen.

He sprawled on the red cushions, his long legs stretched before him and a look of boredom on his handsome face. He was unmistakably Fae, with pointed ears and angular features too perfect to be human. His hair fell past his shoulders in long black waves the same color as his armor. The metal plates hugged his chest and curved over his thighs. One massive hand drummed an armrest, each finger winking with golden rings set with precious gemstones.

Radegast. The Slavic god of hospitality and banqueting.

He sat up as we approached. Around his neck hung a small stone on a black silk cord.

My breath hitched.

His dark gaze fixed on me. "Fyodor," he drawled. "What have you brought me?"

The creature bowed low, the tip of his fluffy hair scraping the stone floor, then positioned himself next to the throne. "A nymph, master. She says she traveled far to see you."

"Really?" Radegast's eyes lit up, the boredom fleeing. He ran an assessing gaze down my body. "Strip and get on the table. You can dance for me while I dine."

I froze, my body going cold then hot. He wanted a stripper?

He put his hands on the arms of his throne and leaned forward. Menace flashed in his eyes. "Remove your clothes or I'll remove your head."

"I…" Panic beat at me. I'd underestimated the danger of the quest.

"Quest?" he asked sharply.

Then his eyes flicked to Hauk.

"Assassin!" Fyodor hissed.

All hell broke loose.

Fyodor screeched.

Hauk ripped his hood back and sprang forward, an obsidian dagger in his hand.

Radegast burst off the throne and flung an arm toward Hauk. "DOWN."

Hauk's knees hit the ground with a sickening crack. The dagger spun out of his hand and clattered on the stone.

I bit back a scream.

Radegast towered over Hauk, his black hair rippling down his back. "You're not the first berserker to come here, you know. The Rage Lords have sent others." He stooped and picked up the dagger—the same one Hauk had worn the day we met in the Hersir's Tower.

Hauk stared up at him with murder in his eyes.

Radegast ran a thumb along the edge, raising a line of blood. "Where did you get this?"

"Nowhere."

Radegast slashed a hand through the air.

Hauk's body jerked backwards, as if something had struck him across the chest. He squeezed his fists at his sides and clenched his jaw.

I stood immobile, fear gripping me like a vise.

"Answer me," Radegast said.

Hauk pressed his lips together, the "fuck you" in his eyes unmistakable.

Radegast's expression darkened. He flicked his hand again.

This time, the blow sent Hauk sprawling. He cried out and grabbed at his chest.

"We can play this game all day," Radegast said in a weary voice.

Hauk stood, his posture defiant.

Radegast made a quick gesture.

Hauk slammed to his knees.

Radegast flicked a glance at me, and I realized he hadn't forgotten me for a second. "My patience grows thin, berserker.

Tell me where you got this dagger or I'll flay the skin from her bones."

"It's volcanic rock," Hauk said at once. "From the Minoan eruption of Thera."

A slow smile spread across Radegast's face. "Quite a long time ago. Bronze Age, yes?"

Hauk was silent, his body as taut as a bowstring.

"Far too long ago for someone like you to have commissioned a weapon like this. There are only a couple like it in the world. The blade is unbreakable. Good for killing demons, wouldn't you agree?"

"Yes."

"You haven't said how you came by it."

Hauk hesitated.

"Shall I fetch a flaying knife?"

"It was my mother's."

"She bought it?"

"She had it made." Hauk bit out each word like it caused him pain. "She commissioned it from a smith who survived the eruption."

Dark satisfaction flooded Radegast's eyes. "A priceless dagger. A warrior mother. A berserker who hunts demons." He let out a low chuckle. "You're Hauk Sigridsson, Crom Cruach's son."

"Which is why you won't kill me."

"Oh?" Radegast put a hand to his breastplate. "Is there some kind of no-killing-of-High-Fae-offspring rule I don't know about?" He turned to Fyodor. "Fyodor, did someone make a new rule like that?"

"Not that I know of, my lord."

Radegast looked at Hauk with a flat expression. "Yeah, we've never heard of that."

Hauk leaned forward, somehow managing to look

dangerous despite his humble position. "My father will rain unholy hell on you if you even think about killing me."

The tension in the great hall climbed several degrees.

Radegast's voice went deadly low. "You think to threaten me?"

The room seemed to rock. I stumbled and almost fell. As I steadied myself, Radegast spoke again.

"I've heard a rumor, Sigridsson, that you've fallen out of favor with Crom. We're isolated here at Nochnaya Krepost, but whispers still come to me. And they say the Crooked One no longer cares what happens to you. That's why he cursed you to stay mortal."

"He did that to teach me a lesson."

Radegast laughed, a booming sound that echoed off the stone. On the banquet table, a basket of rolls tumbled to the floor. "I suppose he cursed you to take on endless quests for the same reason." He sobered and held up the dagger. "You've come to kill me, *da?* Sorry to disappoint, but I can't be killed." He sounded almost...disappointed.

He turned to me, and interest kindled in his gaze. "Fortunately, endless life means endless opportunities to pursue pleasure. Take off your clothes, beauty." He started toward me. "Show me what delights you're hiding. Sigridsson can watch us fuck before he dies."

Hauk raised his voice. "The stone amplifies your magic! You're nothing without it."

Radegast stopped, then slowly turned toward him.

Fear spiked in my chest. Hauk was taunting Radegast to keep him away from me. And now Radegast was going to kill him.

"God of hospitality," Hauk sneered. "You can't even throw a proper party."

"What did you say?"

"I've seen a better banquet at a Holiday Inn."

A choking sound emerged from Radegast's throat.

"*Express*," Hauk added.

Stormclouds gathered in Radegast's eyes. He raised both arms and brought them down in a savage arc.

Hauk flew backwards, smacked hard against the stone wall, and collapsed in a heap.

Radegast stalked toward him, the obsidian dagger clutched in his hand.

I didn't think. I just sucked in a breath and yelled, "Hey, Radegast!"

He whirled around, death in his eyes.

I pulled my shirt over my head and unhooked my bra. Topless, I put my hands on my hips and offered him a coy smile. "What was that you said about pleasure?"

R adegast's gaze went straight to my breasts.

Can it really be this easy?

His dark brows pulled together. "What's easy?"

My pulse spiked. Quickly, I pictured a thick wall in my head. "Getting to know you," I said, plastering a smile on my face and lifting a casual shoulder. "I heard you like nymphs, so I had to come visit."

He kept his eyes glued to my chest. His lips parted, and his breaths grew labored.

Crom's voice ran through my head. *"He likes to play with his food."*

My nipples puckered in fear.

Radegast groaned.

Setting aside every ounce of pride I possessed, I rolled my shoulders back, making my breasts bounce gently.

He stepped toward me—and away from Hauk.

"My lord!" Fyodor protested from his spot near the throne. "She came with the berserker. They could be working together."

Eyes on me, Radegast waved him off. "Hush, Fyodor."

"But she could be dangerous!"

Radegast's mouth twisted. He spun and slashed a hand through the air. A red gash opened across Fyodor's chest. For a moment, he stood there, looking down at himself with a bemused expression as blood poured from the wound. Then he crumpled to the ground, his eyes sightless.

I breathed through my nose as nausea burned my throat.

Radegast turned back to me with an indulgent smile. "Don't worry about him," he said, closing the distance between us. He reached me and dropped his eyes to my breasts. "Nymphs are the least dangerous creatures in Faerie," he murmured, then proffered his arm in a courtly gesture.

I rested my fingertips on his gauntleted forearm and let him lead me to the banquet table. Smile frozen on my face, I climbed the dais and made a murmur of gratitude as he pulled out a chair. The table was laden with enough food to serve two dozen guests. A long strip of evergreen garland ran down the center, its green needles decorated with pinecones and holly berries. It was beautiful and festive—and a sharp contrast to the murderous High Fae settling his large body in the chair next to mine.

He removed his gauntlets and ran a possessive finger down my breast. "Lose the trousers, pet. I'm eager to sample your charms."

My heart fluttered wildly.

His eyes narrowed. "I don't like to be kept waiting, nymph."

A bird's caw echoed through the hall, making me jump.

Radegast turned as a black missile streaked through the air and settled at the far end of the table. "A raven," he said, his voice thick with disdain. "They get in through the chimneys.

Messy, disgusting creatures, shitting all over the place." He slammed a fist down. "Get!"

The bird hopped in place and cocked its head.

My breath caught. Its eyes were blue...

It spread its wings and launched into the air, swooping toward Radegast's throne.

The staff leaned against it, the tip just visible.

Radegast cupped my jaw and turned my head back to him. "Ignore the bird," he said, his breaths ragged. "Undress. I ache to see the rest of you."

"I... Let's wait."

He frowned. "There's something strange about you. The other nymphs I've met skipped nude through my halls and begged for my touch. You said you came in with Sigridsson?" He started to swivel toward Hauk.

"M-My lord!" I extended my arms over my head and stretched, arching my spine.

He fastened his gaze to my chest, the tip of a red tongue wetting his lips. "What is it?" he asked absently.

I deepened my stretch and made my voice breathless. "I almost forgot...I brought you a gift."

"A present?"

"It's customary to offer one's host a gift, yes?"

"Yes, of course." He sighed. "But so few remember the old ways."

I lowered my arms and leaned toward him. "I remembered. Do you mind if I go fetch it"—I leaned closer, and his gaze tracked the sway of my breasts—"my lord?"

"Where is it?"

I pointed a languid finger toward the throne. "Just there. I'll rush right back to you."

"By all means."

I stood and left the dais. The second I was clear of it, I cast an anxious glance at Hauk. He still lay unconscious, but his chest rose and fell.

I grabbed the staff and started back to the table. The wood hummed under my hand.

And I *changed*.

My movements became more fluid and graceful. My hair floated around my shoulders. My breasts grew heavier, my nipples taut and tingling. A glance down revealed they were darker, the pink bold and alluring. Tiny green vines spread under my skin, the leaves glowing like they were lit from within. Power—raw and wild—snapped at my heels and crackled over my skin.

Radegast's eyes glittered with hunger as I approached. "My lady nymph," he growled.

"My lord," I purred. I tossed my hair over my shoulder as I climbed the dais. "I have your gift."

He snagged me around the waist and pulled me onto his lap so I straddled him, my breasts brushing his chest. "*You* are the gift." He snatched the staff from my grip and lay it across the table.

I bit back a curse. "Don't you want to see it?" He was so large, my feet dangled on either side of his thighs.

"Later." He traced a vine that swirled down my neck. "These markings... Unconventional, but I find them very"—his breath hitched—"erotic."

I gritted my teeth, my gaze on the stone resting against his breastplate. He wore it right out in the open? Maybe it wasn't the real one.

"The real what?" he murmured, his fingers wandering lower.

"N-Nothing."

He dipped his head toward my nipple.

I slapped a hand against his breastplate, stopping his descent. "Wait."

"I've waited long enough," he rasped. His fingers went to the button of my pants.

The raven burst into the air, croaking loudly.

Radegast pounded the table. "Begone, you pest!"

My heart beat faster.

He turned back to me. "My apologies."

Before he could go for my pants again, I touched his cheek. "We haven't dined. The food grows cold. And"—I trailed my fingers down his neck and traced a path over his breastplate— "I've heard your banquets have the most delicious food in the world. I've traveled far to be with you, and I'm starved. Could we eat before we have our fun?" My fingertips brushed the stone.

He straightened, and it shifted out of my reach. "You're right. A good host never lets his guests go hungry." He lifted me by the waist and spun me around on his lap.

I clutched at the table's edge, dizzy from the unexpected movement.

He pulled a serving dish toward us and spooned food onto a platter. "You must try this, my lady, and tell me what you think."

The scent of onions and peppers hit my nose. It was some kind of pasta dish with big, round noodles.

He lifted the spoon as if he would feed me. "It's *makaroni po flotski*."

My gaze caught on something...

Those aren't noodles.

They were human fingers.

Nausea choked me. Hauk was right. No wonder the Rage Lords wanted him dead.

He moved so quickly, I didn't have a chance to react. He

surged up, grabbed my shoulders, and slammed me face first onto the table. While I was still struggling to catch my breath, he flipped me over and seized my throat. His fingers squeezed, and his enraged face filled my vision. The stone swung on its cord.

"The Rage Lords?" he thundered. His fingers tightened.

I wheezed, fighting for oxygen. The tendons in my neck began to give...

"They sent a *nymph* to try to kill me?"

White-hot pain streaked through me. As my eyes began to bulge, I sucked in a breath. "Not try," I gasped. "Did." I snatched the stone from his neck.

His face froze in a stunned expression. A sucking sound emerged from his throat. He tightened his grip, his fingers choking off my air completely.

My head swam. My legs trembled as my body fought unconsciousness.

He continued wheezing. Little black veins crisscrossed his cheeks and forehead. His lips turned bright red.

My vision dimmed. Distantly, I heard a raven croak.

Hauk reared behind Radegast, his eyes forked with lightning, his mouth open on a warrior's bellow. He plunged the obsidian dagger into the side of Radegast's neck.

Blood sprayed. Radegast lurched—his face still locked in a choking gasp—and crashed to the ground.

Hauk fell on his body. He pulled the dagger free and swung it in a vicious arc, decapitating Radegast in a single blow.

I pushed myself upright and clutched at the table.

Hauk stood over Radegast, his chest heaving. He closed his eyes on a long blink. When he opened them, they were blue once more.

He turned toward me. "Elin?"

"Hauk," I rasped, the pain in my throat like razor blades. I held up the stone. "I got it."

His eyes widened. A smile spread over his face.

The air behind him went wavy. Nils stepped out of a portal with a broadsword in his hand.

Hauk frowned. Started to turn—

Nils flipped his blade and brought the hilt down on Hauk's head.

I froze, complete and utter shock consuming me.

For a moment, Hauk remained upright. He stared at me, his face almost comically confused. Then his eyes rolled back in his head, and he slumped to the ground.

CHAPTER
TWENTY-TWO

For a moment, Nils and I stared at Hauk.

Then our eyes locked.

I charged down the dais. "What the *fuck!*"

He stepped back and put up his free hand. "Easy, Elin, I didn't kill him!"

I rushed to Hauk and knelt. He lay on his side, blood pooling under his head. I pressed my fingers to his neck. His pulse was steady, and I exhaled in relief.

"He's fine," Nils said above me. "It takes a lot more than a blow like that to kill a berserker."

I surged to my feet. "What are you doing here? Why did you hit him?"

"I followed you."

"Obviously," I said through clenched teeth. "How did you find this place?"

He hesitated. "Your mirror. Harald had the witch who made it put a tracking spell on it."

Shock left me speechless. He'd given me the mirror as a child... Why would he want to track me?

"Sigridsson doesn't care about you." Anger flashed in Nils' eyes. "Gods, Elin, he brought you here to whore for Radegast. And just look at you!"

I glanced down at myself. In the struggle with Radegast, I'd forgotten about being topless. Tossing Nils a dark look, I went to my shirt and yanked it over my head. I shoved the stone in my pocket.

He drifted toward me. "Don't be that way, Elin. I came here because I love you."

"Loving someone doesn't give you the right to interfere in their life. I came with Hauk because I wanted to."

His jaw set. "I don't believe that."

The air next to him rippled. Harald stepped into the hall with a drawn sword.

I sucked in a breath and scanned the air around him, braced for the other Rage Lords to appear.

Nils turned to him and made a short bow. "Radegast is dead, my lord. And I incapacitated Sigridsson."

Harald clapped him on the shoulder. "Excellent, Nils. You've served your purpose." He pulled his sword back and plunged it in Nils' stomach.

I clapped my hands over my mouth, horror pounding through me.

Nils bent in half, his eyes wide with shock. Blood bubbled on his lips as he gasped, "Why?"

Harald sighed. "I had such high hopes for you."

Nils fell to his knees. "You said I could...have her."

"And in that, you turned out just like your father. Chasing after a woman unworthy of your regard." Harald put a boot on his shoulder and shoved. Nils crashed to his side.

"No!" I rushed forward.

Harald whipped toward me and extended his sword. "Not another step."

I stopped, hot tears splashing down my cheeks.

Nils made a choking sound. Blood spread in a circle around him. His lips trembled as his gaze met mine. "Elin. I'm so... sorry." His mouth went slack, his eyes empty and unseeing.

Wrath seared my veins. With a strangled cry, I flew at Harald.

He backhanded me across the face.

Pain exploded in my cheek. The force of the blow spun me around, but I stayed on my feet. When I turned back, he watched me with cold eyes.

"You *killed* him," I shouted.

"He was a fool." He put out his hand. "Now give me the stone."

I caught my breath. Was *that* why he'd followed me? He wanted the Eternity Stone? "I don't have it," I said.

Irritation crossed his face. "Don't be stupid, Elin."

I held his stare.

He waited a moment, then turned and walked to Hauk.

Alarm bolted through me. "Wait!"

He stopped with the tip of his bloodied sword hovering over Hauk's body. "Give me the stone or I put a sword through his heart."

He would. The promise was there in his gaze. I could resurrect Hauk, but not before Harald killed me, too.

I pulled the stone from my pocket and walked over. "You promise you won't hurt him?"

"You have my word."

I held out the stone.

He took it and slipped it into his pocket.

Then he shoved his sword into Hauk's chest.

My world froze. Shattered.

I shattered, too, my being crumbling into a million pieces.

Hauk's eyes flew open. His face contorted in agony. He

looked at Harald, and his lips moved. Before he could speak, blood flowed from his mouth.

Harald stared down at him, his expression blank. Dispassionate. With a savage twist, he wrenched the sword from Hauk's chest. Blood pumped like a fountain.

Mortal. He was mortal.

I dropped to my knees and slapped my hands over the wound. "No! Hauk, look at me."

His hand lifted. Brushed my cheek. "Elin."

"Don't talk." I pressed hard. Blood seeped around my hands, the flow growing faster. "Stay still and we'll—"

"Elin. Stop."

I looked up and found him smiling at me, his blue eyes wistful. "You were so brave today. I wish..." He lapsed into a coughing fit, foamy blood flecking his lips.

"Hauk!" I clutched his shoulders. Tears streamed down my face.

He calmed. When he found my gaze this time, he squinted, as if he had trouble seeing me. His chest rattled, and his voice fell to a whisper. "I wish we'd had more time. We could have been"—a tear slipped from the corner of his eye and streaked into his hair—"perfect." His chest lifted...fell. And stopped.

For a second, I couldn't move. I stared at him, denial holding me in place. He couldn't die. He was Crom's son. He was the Hersir.

He was mine.

"Touching," Harald said above me.

Slowly, I looked up. The devastation in my heart shifted, replaced with cold, all-consuming fury.

I stood and faced him over Hauk's body. "You didn't have to kill him," I said, my voice oddly calm in my ears. "I gave you the stone."

"He would have talked."

"The High Fae will hunt you. They want the stone returned to Faerie."

His smile was cruel. "So they'll send a berserker after me?" He gestured to Hauk. "If this was their best, I have nothing to worry about." He leaned over and wiped his sword on Hauk's body.

"You *fucking* asshole!" I screamed. "Don't you touch him!"

He straightened, the contempt in his eyes searing me to my soul. He stepped over Hauk. In a voice seething with quiet menace, he asked, "And who's going to stop me? You?"

I stumbled back. "So you're going to kill me now, too?"

He stopped, and his face twisted with so much hate it stole my breath. "If only I could," he spat. Words spilled from him like puss seeping from an infected wound. "I tried to make you do it yourself, to rid me of this burden I've dragged around for twenty-one years. But you couldn't even do that."

My heart thumped, and a sense of foreboding settled over me, making shivers rush over my skin. "What are you talking about?"

"You really are as silly and empty-headed as the rest of your race, aren't you? Everyone around you has died and you haven't figured it out. So let me spell it out for you. I killed them all. One by one. The maid who used to sing you to sleep. That stupid Brownie you clung to like a leech. The old Selkie butler. Your slut of a mother."

The ball formed in an instant.

Rage.

I *seethed* with it.

"You were supposed to be powerful," he spat. "But you're nothing but a nymph. Worse, you lack even the most basic Fae magic. I gave you my name and the protection of my house. In return, you've brought me shame and embarrassment. You could have at least made yourself useful in Einar's bed. But you couldn't even do that right."

It was nothing—no struggle at all—to extend my hand and beckon my staff.

"COME," I told it, and the wood lifted from the table and smacked into my palm.

Wild, wicked magic rolled through me. The ancient music of forests and fields. *Power.*

I seethed with that, too. My rage and my magic slid over each other, no longer at odds.

Now, they joined.

Vines snaked under my skin, scurrying down my limbs until I glowed with green.

The staff pulsed under my hand—ready and waiting. Smooth as silk, the ball of rage in my chest flowed down my arm and into the wood.

Harald's eyes widened. For a brief moment, fear flickered in the pale depths.

I pointed the staff at him.

He lifted his sword. "I have the stone. I can't be killed."

"We'll see about that." I flicked the staff.

He flew across the room and smashed into the banquet table.

The evergreen garland moved sinuously, curving toward him like a snake. *"My lady. I am yours to command."*

I pointed the staff at Harald. "This one."

The garland shivered and swept toward him.

He sprang up and whirled, his gaze on the garland. "What foul magic is this?"

I walked forward, my hair floating about my shoulders. "Hold him," I told the evergreen.

The garland swept around his waist like a tentacle and slammed him back to the table. As he sprawled, the green length circled his body over and over, wrapping tightly around his arms, his legs, his torso. Needles pierced his skin. He arched and screamed.

I stood with my feet braced apart, the garland's hisses like music in my ears.

Harald writhed. "You stupid nymph whore! Your plants can't harm me! I have the Eternity Stone." He managed to shift his hand. The stone gleamed between his curled fingers.

I rested the tip of the staff on the ground. "I've taken it from one man today. I think I'll make it two for two."

His gaze went to the staff, and terror shone in his eyes. Then he focused on me. "You can't kill me. I'm your father."

A raven hopped onto his shoulder. It stared at me a moment, then lifted into the air and sailed high overhead, black wings spread.

Then it wheeled and plunged toward me.

And changed shape.

One minute, the bird swooped at me. The next, a man with waist-length white hair stepped onto the flagstones. He was neither young nor old, and he carried power around him like a cloak. He wore a black patch over his right eye. The left was a pale blue. His feet were bare, and gold bracelets climbed up his forearms. A platinum-blond beard covered his jaw, small silver beads tucked here and there in the mass.

He towered over me, even taller than Radegast. His warrior's body rippled with muscle, and the broadsword strapped to his side glowed with blue fire.

He was larger than life, Odin the All-Father. The missing god.

Returned at last.

He looked at Harald with eyes that were beautiful and terrible. "You are not her father, Harald Berregaard. That honor belongs to me."

TWENTY-THREE

I stared at Odin.

I couldn't have heard him right.

A smile touched his lips. "Come now, Elin." He held his arms away from his body. "Look closer."

We stared at each other. A beat of recognition thumped inside me, like someone had plucked a lute in my soul.

"You know me," he said, his deep voice soft.

The lute vibrated again. A tear slipped down my cheek.

"What will you do with him?" he asked.

"He killed my mother."

Pain—there and gone—flashed in his pale blue eye. "And others."

I swallowed hard. "How could you let that happen?"

His voice grew solemn. "I don't control fate. That is the domain of the Norns."

"I don't believe that. We all have free will."

He smiled, and it made his face young. "That we do." He glanced at the staff in my hand. "And what a strong will it takes to bend one's fate."

Silence fell. I drew a deep breath. "Why did you leave me alone?"

The mighty chest rose and fell in a sigh. "It is a difficult thing to be the child of a god. History gives us examples of those who suffered greatly for it. And I didn't desert you. I sent friends and helpers. Fiona the Brownie to teach you tenderness. Asher Greenleaf to show you the power of living things." He looked at Nils' body. "That one to show you that true love is more than lust."

An ache shot through my heart. "Can you bring him back?"

He looked at me, Odin the All-Father. My father. "I cannot, daughter." He touched the patch over his eye. "I sacrificed much to learn what lies beyond. Not even I can venture there. And those who sail to those lands can't return."

"His death was senseless."

Odin shook his head. "He died exactly how he was supposed to."

"What about my mother? Was she supposed to die the way she did?"

Lightning flashed in his good eye. He turned to Harald. "I gave Caitríona Greenleaf into your care for safekeeping, along with the child I got on her."

Held tight by the evergreen, Harald snarled. "And I was promised immortality in return!"

"You should have been patient, Berregaard."

"How long was I supposed to wait?" Harald turned hateful eyes to me. "And your child brought nothing but dishonor to my house. Her rage burns out of control. She's unfocused and weak."

Odin put a large hand on my shoulder. "She is the daughter of lightning. When she draws power, she pulls it directly from Asgard. It will take her centuries to master it."

Harald's gaze widened. Then he made a scoffing sound, as if he was unimpressed.

He really was *such* a bitch.

Odin spoke again, and now there was thunder in his voice. "But you still haven't answered for the nymph. She was special to me, and her child more so. You took a life that was not yours to take."

I tensed. He called my mother "the nymph" as if she'd been nothing more than a fling.

He turned to me. "She was my beloved for a time. Her love was freely given, as was mine." He brushed my cheek—the one Harald had struck. As his hand moved over my skin, the pain faded. He smiled. "You are as lovely as she was. And just as Crom called you. Daughter of rage and beauty."

The mention of Crom made me look around Odin to where Hauk lay. As my gaze fell on his lifeless body, a tight fist squeezed my heart.

Odin spoke quietly. "Caitríona told you I approached. I am here now. You have a choice to make."

The stone.

My mother had known.

"Yes," Odin said. "She bent the rules so she could warn you." He gave a little shrug. "Mothers tend to get special passes for that sort of thing."

The fist around my heart tightened. I could resurrect my mother, or I could resurrect Hauk.

I couldn't do both.

Odin's voice was gentle. "Easy decisions first. What will you do with Berregaard?"

I looked at Harald, who glared at me from his evergreen prison. He'd murdered everyone I cared about.

I walked forward. Odin advanced with me.

"No!" Harald writhed in the vines, jerking his limbs. "I can't be killed! I have the stone!"

The staff heated under my hand, which glowed with a hundred tiny vines. I walked up to Harald and plucked the Eternity Stone from his grip. "Now you don't."

I returned to Odin's side and faced Harald.

"You can't!" he screamed. "I was promised immortality!"

I looked at the evergreen. "Kill him."

The garland shivered. *"My lady."* It shivered again and dipped toward Odin. *"My lord."*

Odin returned the bow, his good eye streaked with bolts of lightning.

Harald thrashed and screamed louder.

The garland tightened around his throat, silencing his cries. Needles pierced his skin in a thousand places. He gurgled, his features twisting in agony.

"Finish it," I ordered.

The garland jerked. A thick red line appeared like a smile around Harald's neck. There was a sharp crack, and his head fell back onto the table.

For a moment, Odin and I stood silent.

Then my hand heated up. I lifted it and opened my palm.

Odin and I stared at the Eternity Stone in the center of my hand.

"Such a small thing," he said, "to cause so much trouble."

"I thought it would look different."

He smiled. "It takes various forms depending on who's looking at it. To Radegast, it was a heavy gemstone set in gold. To the humans who used it to bring back a loved one who ran afoul of the Roman authorities, it was a boulder big enough to cover a tomb."

I closed my hand over it.

"Have you made your choice?" Odin asked.

"Yes."

"Be quick about it," he urged. "The stone corrupts."

I went to Hauk and knelt by his side. He was still, his body cold.

I had no idea what to do next. "Um...Odin?"

He walked over, his bare feet silent on the flagstones. "You can call me Dad, you know. Most of your half-siblings do."

I bit my lip. "Thanks...but I might need some time to get used to it."

He nodded. "Just tell the stone what you want it to do. Don't elaborate. With magic, simple and to the point is best."

I looked at the stone and took a deep breath. "I want Hauk Sigridsson to be alive again."

Nothing happened.

My heart sank. After everything, it didn't work. It was just a stupid rock—

Hauk's eyes flew open.

I fell on my ass.

Odin laughed.

Hauk sucked in a huge breath and sat up. "Elin?"

I threw my arms around him, nearly tackling him to the ground. "You're back!"

His arms came around me slowly. "Back?" he asked, his voice bewildered. "Did I go somewhere?"

I pulled away and put my hands on his face. "I thought I lost you."

The stunned look faded from his eyes as the color returned to his cheeks. He covered my hands with his, his gaze full of wonder. "You saved me. You used the stone."

Abruptly, I realized I didn't have it anymore. I looked up, my gaze colliding with Odin's.

"It's gone," he said. "Returned to Faerie, where it can't cause any more mischief. At least for a time."

Which meant Hauk couldn't use it, I thought, my heart sinking. He'd stay mortal, trapped in Crom's curse.

Odin waved a hand. "I'm more powerful than Crom. And I want my daughter to be with the man she loves." He looked at Hauk. "The curse is lifted, Sigridsson. Your immortality is restored."

Hauk stared at Odin, his face pale again. "Is that..." He looked at me. "Daughter?"

"Yes," I said. "And it's a long story."

For a moment, he seemed speechless. Then a slow grin spread across his face. "So you love me, huh?"

I rolled my eyes. "Now I *know* you're okay."

He leaned toward me, his gaze gleaming with a mix of humor and heat. "Well if you're going to bring me back from the dead, at least do it with a kiss."

"That's Sleeping Beauty," I said as he drew near. "And the prince is supposed to kiss the princess, not the other way around."

"I like this way better," he murmured, then pressed his lips to mine.

EPILOGUE

I woke with a wicked tongue swirling around my clit.

My eyes flew open and my breath left me in a rush. Morning sunlight spilled across the bed, filling the room with a warm, yellow glow.

But it was nothing compared to the heat building between my legs.

As I arched my back, the sheet slipped below my breasts. The air teased my nipples, which throbbed in sync with my racing heart.

"So that dream I was just having wasn't a dream after all," I murmured.

The sheet lifted, and Hauk rose from between my thighs. His blond hair spilled around his shoulders, and his eyes were hooded with lust. He wiped his glistening mouth with the back of his hand and gave me a smug smile. "I'm the dream, baby. Day and night."

I lifted my arm and pointed down. "Finish what you started."

"Yes, ma'am." He winked and lowered his head. His hot

tongue licked up my folds, and then he sucked my clit into his mouth.

I threaded the fingers of one hand through his hair and held him against my sex as pleasure coiled tight in my core.

He worked me faster, licking and sucking. Filling the room with his husky moans and the wet sounds of his mouth on my sodden sex. The coil of pleasure tightened further, my breaths coming in short, whimpering pants. My muscles tensed and then the coil sprung open, flinging me in every direction.

He slowed his kisses as I came, lapping softly at my opening. When I finally sighed, my body limp and sated, he climbed up the bed and rolled me into his arms.

"Good morning," he murmured, his chin brushing the top of my head.

I closed my eyes on a contented smile. "A *very* good morning."

He chuckled and reached around my body to play with one of my nipples. "So you were dreaming about me?" he asked, his fingers stroking the taut peak.

"I never said I was dreaming about *you*," I answered lazily.

He gave me a light pinch. "But you were."

I made a non-committal sound.

"You can't lie anymore, love." He drew teasing circles, stoking fresh desire.

He was right, and it was a massive inconvenience. Odin (it was still weird to think of him as my father) had explained that my non-existent glamour wasn't so non-existent after all. He'd hobbled it when I was an infant to keep my identity a secret— and so I'd be forced to grow up without my full range of powers. With my magic muffled, I'd lacked the abilities that were my birthright. But I'd also been free to lie when the need arose. It was going to take a while to adjust to my new reality.

"Do you forgive him?" Hauk asked softly, guessing the direction of my thoughts.

I turned in his arms and met his gaze. "I...don't know. I understand his reasons for wanting me to grow up as anonymously as possible. He was worried I'd let my parentage go to my head. But he didn't have to leave me with Harald. He wanted to make me tough. But I grew up being hated and not knowing why."

Hauk spoke carefully, as if he wanted to get every word just right. "I understand more than most how having a High Fae for a parent can lead to one seriously fucked up childhood. But you can't think of Odin as a normal dad. He's lived for thousands of years, and he's as close to being a true immortal as anyone can get without possessing the Eternity Stone. You lived under Harald's roof for twenty-one years. That's nothing to someone who's lived a hundred lifetimes."

"So he expects me to forget what happened and start showing up for family dinners in Asgard?"

Hauk smoothed my hair away from my forehead. "No," he said gently, "but my guess is he assumes he's got plenty of time to make things up to you. Whether you accept his version of an apology or not is your choice, sweetheart. It's always your choice."

I touched his jaw. "Do you think you'll ever get an apology from Crom?"

"No. And it's okay if I can't forgive him. That's a choice, too. Maybe it'll come with time...maybe not. Either way, I don't need to decide right now." He turned his head and kissed my fingers. "I've got everything I need to be happy."

My stomach fluttered. "Hauk Sigridsson, are you saying I make you happy?"

"Happy. Hard. Confused. Horny."

I couldn't control my grin. "I think hard and horny are the same thing."

"Oh no. They're different, trust me." He sat up with a twinkle in his eyes. "I almost forgot. I have something for you." He bounded out of bed and across the bedroom before I could say anything.

I settled back on the pillows and enjoyed the view of six-and-a-half feet of naked berserker as he bent over the desk on the far side of the room. If any sight could rival the Eiffel Tower outside the window, it was his taut, muscled ass. We'd returned to the Paris apartment after the quest because we'd both needed rest and quiet. That had been six months ago, and neither of us felt like leaving. The place was small, but it was perfect for the two of us.

Then again, we spent most of our time in bed.

Hauk returned with a wooden box, which he set next to me.

"What is it?" I asked.

He lay on his side with his head on his hand. "That's for me to know and you to find out."

Smiling, I lifted the lid—and gasped.

A leather-bound book lay inside, its cover engraved with lines of golden runes.

The Saga of Elin the Unyielding

Berserker

Nymph

Daughter of Rage and Beauty

"Unyielding," I murmured.

"That was Asher's idea," Hauk said. "Something about steel that bends without breaking."

My throat burned. "I got my own saga."

"Take it out and have a look."

I lifted the book and ran my fingertips over the gold lettering. "I never thought..." I cleared my throat as I blinked back tears. "I didn't expect to show up in one of these, let alone get a whole book to myself."

"You got the stone from Radegast."

I looked up at Hauk. "But you killed him."

He winked. "I have a chapter or two."

Heat flared in all the usual places, and I ducked my head and flipped through the book so he wouldn't realize how powerless I was to resist his winks. As the pages flashed by, I frowned. "This is half empty."

He chuckled and lifted my gaze with a warm hand under my chin. His blue eyes flickered with silver—a sure sign he knew exactly how much his winks affected me. "We have to fill them, love. But don't worry, we've got lots of time."

My breath hitched. "Forever?"

He set the book aside and drew me into his arms. "Absolutely forever," he murmured, then sealed his promise with a kiss.

∾

ABOUT THE AUTHOR

Amy Pennza is a USA Today Bestselling Author of steamy paranormal and contemporary romance. After stints as a lawyer and a soldier, she discovered her dream job is writing about stubborn alphas and smart heroines. She lives in the Great Lakes region with her husband and five children.

Keep up with new releases by visiting amypennza.com

Want exclusive goodies like free books and fun giveaways? Sign up for Amy's newsletter at www.amypennza.com/subscribe

ALSO BY AMY PENNZA

Check out all my books by clicking here.

And if you love wolf shifters, don't miss my ultra-steamy Lux Catena Series. Each book can be read as a standalone.

What a Wolf Desires

What a Wolf Dares

What a Wolf Demands

What a Wolf's Heart Decides

Lux Catena Series Shifter Romance Box Set

www.ingramcontent.com/pod-product-compliance
Lightning Source LLC
Chambersburg PA
CBHW020239130626
46549CB00005B/1976